Cat among the Pigeons

JULIA GOLDING

THE SECOND BOOK FROM
CAT ROYAL

EGMONT

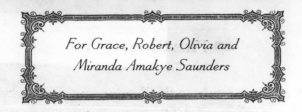

For Grace, Robert, Olivia and
Miranda Amakye Saunders

Bowles's New Plan of London map courtesy of the British Library

EGMONT
We bring stories to life

First published 2006
by Egmont UK Ltd
239 Kensington High Street, London W8 6SA

Copyright © 2006 Julia Golding
Cover illustration copyright © Tim Spencer 2006

The moral rights of the author and cover illustrator have been asserted

ISBN 978 1 4052 2423 9
ISBN 1 4052 2423 1

1 3 5 7 9 10 8 6 4 2

A CIP catalogue record for this title is available from the
British Library

Printed and bound in Great Britain by the CPI Group

Egmont
Press
is committed to
Ethical
Publishing

www.egmont.co.uk/ethicalpublishing

❧ THE CRITICS ❧

'A welcome return to the London stage for Drury Lane's favourite child' – JOHN PHILIP KEMBLE

'Cat Royal's prose grips the reader like an ancient mariner intent on telling you his tale (now there's an idea . . .)' – SAMUEL TAYLOR COLERIDGE

'Starched small linen all morning, admired daffodils with William, read Cat Royal with great pleasure in evening' – DOROTHY WORDSWORTH, *extract from her journal*

'Cat Royal serves no utilitarian function whatsoever – clearly a case for the poorhouse' – JEREMY BENTHAM

'I have forbidden my children to read this pernicious stuff!' – H. M. QUEEN CHARLOTTE

'Cat Royal gives us quite a giggle' – DOROTHY JORDAN AND H.R.H. THE DUKE OF CLARENCE

'I'm sure Cat Royal must be a fake dreamt up by an educated gentleman!' – JAMES 'OSSIAN' MACPHERSON

'Fit only for the bonfire' – THE SOCIETY OF
GENTLEMEN PLANTERS, JAMAICA

'Her work is music to my ears!' – LUDWIG VAN
BEETHOVEN

'Degenerate stuff – enough to cause a mutiny!'
– CAPTAIN WILLIAM BLIGH, *late of the Bounty*

'Her pen paints a picture better than a brush'
– SIR JOSHUA REYNOLDS

'Not enough Scotsmen for my taste'
– WALTER SCOTT

'A book that every right-thinking person in this
nation of slave traders should read and reflect
upon' – WILLIAM WILBERFORCE

❧ A Note to the Reader ❧

If you have not yet read the first instalment of my adventures, *The Diamond of Drury Lane*, there are a few things you need to know. In that book, I explained how I made friends with Pedro Hawkins, a former slave from Africa, during an eventful balloon ride in Drury Lane. I recounted how, after Pedro's theatrical triumph, we became acquainted with the two children of the Duke of Avon: Lord Francis and Lady Elizabeth (Frank and Lizzie to you). Together we saved a cartooning rebel lord from the gallows and I narrowly escaped death myself. Unfortunately, in the course of my adventures I managed to make myself the enemy of Billy Shepherd, a ruthless gang leader. Something told me even then that I hadn't heard the last of him. If you want to find out what happened next, read on.

Catherine 'Cat' Royal

INDEX

PRINCIPAL CHARACTERS

IN THE THEATRE

MISS CATHERINE 'CAT' ROYAL – ward of the theatre

MR PEDRO HAWKINS – talented musician, a former slave under threat of recapture

MR SHERIDAN – playwright, politician, theatre owner

MR KEMBLE – actor-manager, best Shakespearean actor in the world

SIGNOR ANGELINI – musical director who thinks he is Pedro's master

COVENT GARDEN MARKET

MR SYD FLETCHER – boxer, leader of the Butcher's Boys

MR BILLY SHEPHERD – leader of rival gang who thinks he's going up in the world

JOE 'THE CARD' MURRAY – one of Syd's boys, street magician

THE DUKE'S HOUSEHOLD

LORD FRANCIS, OR FRANK – reluctant schoolboy, heir to a dukedom, master forger

LADY ELIZABETH, OR LIZZIE – his sister, who is annoying her mother by refusing to elope

DUCHESS OF AVON – Lizzie and Frank's mother, the peeress, formerly the singer known as The Bristol Nightingale

WESTMINSTER SCHOOL

THE HONORABLE CHARLES HENGRAVE, OR CHARLIE – a good sport and great friend

DR VINCENT – the headmaster, very attached to his cane

MR CASTLETON – theatrically minded Latin master

MR RICHMOND – runty offspring of slave plantation owner

MR INGELS – his none-too-bright sidekick

THE ABOLITIONISTS

MR OLAUDAH EQUIANO – former slave, great traveller, leading light of abolition movement

MR GRANVILLE SHARP – legal brains behind abolitionists

THE MISS MILLERS (PATIENCE, PRUDENCE AND
FORTITUDE) – kind Quakers with an
unexpectedly powerful grip

MISS MILLY HENGRAVE – sister to Charlie with
a talent for saying the wrong thing

THE SLAVERS

MR KINGSTON HAWKINS – Pedro's old master
and a nasty piece of work

Actors, ballerinas, scandalized gentlemen,
rioting schoolboys, et al.

Julia Golding

Julia Golding read English at Cambridge then joined the Foreign Office and served in Poland. Her work as a diplomat took her from the high point of town twinning in the Tatra Mountains to the low of inspecting the bottom of a Silesian coal mine.

On leaving Poland, she exchanged diplomacy for academia and took a doctorate in the literature of the English Romantic Period at Oxford. She then joined Oxfam as a lobbyist on conflict issues, campaigning at the UN and with governments to lessen the impact of conflict on civilians living in war zones.

Married with three children, Julia now lives in Oxford and works as a freelance writer. CAT AMONG THE PIGEONS is the sequel to the brilliant THE DIAMOND OF DRURY LANE, winner of the Ottakar's Children's Book prize 2006.

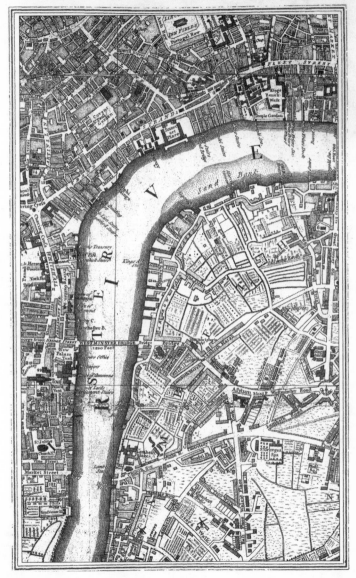

PROLOGUE

RETURN OF THE MASTER

I still can't believe it happened – not here, not in my theatre.

Forgive my scrawl: my hands are shaking even as I write this. I find it hard to put pen to paper when I want to scream at the unfairness of the world and throw the inkpot across the room. Oh yes, we Londoners pretend to be all civilized and cultured, a beacon to the world, but it's all lies. We're rotten – and will remain so as long as a man is able to walk into the Theatre Royal, Drury Lane, and claim a fellow human being as his property.

I must calm myself.

Part of it is my fault for I told Pedro that we

would have the place to ourselves this early in the morning; I thought we'd have plenty of time to practise away from hostile eyes. How wrong I was.

You see, Reader, Pedro has just been cast in his first speaking role: that of Ariel, the sprite who serves the magician Prospero in Shakespeare's *The Tempest*. I am so proud of him – and of Mr Kemble who has taken a gamble in giving the role to Pedro over the heads of many more experienced actors. There had been quite a rumpus backstage when the news leaked out to the cast that one of the choice roles had gone to my African friend. It wasn't enough for some of the disappointed actors that he had proved himself a skilled musician and a dancer – to them he is still an outsider and he's black-skinned: that damns him in their eyes. With the lingering jealousy and prejudice backstage, Pedro wanted to prove his detractors wrong and be word perfect for the dress rehearsal today.

'Come on, Pedro, give me a hand here!' I put my lantern on the floor and struggled with the winch that raises the curtains. Pedro was standing motionless on the forestage, staring into the darkness of the empty auditorium. Doubtless he was imagining a variety of receptions for his debut. Would it be orange peel and turnips or flowers and applause?

'Stop thinking about it,' I cautioned him. 'What will happen will happen. Nobody, not even Mr Sheridan himself, can guess how an audience will behave on the night.'

Pedro turned to me and flashed a brilliant smile. The light of his candle lit him alone, leaving the rest of the theatre in darkness. 'They're going to be amazed.' He threw his arms wide and bowed. 'I'll make sure they love me!'

'Hmm, we'll see.' I'd forgotten that Pedro was never one to underestimate his own abilities. 'If you're going to be so astonishing, we'd better practise some more. Give a lady a hand, will you?'

Pedro took the other side of the winch and we turned it together, lifting the heavy red drapes as if we were furling a sail.

'*Blow the man down, bully,*

Blow the man down,' Pedro began to sing.

I joined in.

'*With a way, hey,*

Blow the man down.'

By the end of the verse the curtains were stowed and we had the whole stage to play on.

'We'll need some more light, or one of us is going to end up in the orchestra with a broken neck,' I said, crouching over the footlights to coax them into life with a taper.

'Not me. I think I could act on this stage blindfold,' boasted Pedro. He lit a second taper and began at the other end. Exchanging a glance, we raced to see who could reach the middle first. I won. At least I was still better at some things than my accomplished friend.

'There, that's done.' I stood up. 'Let's start from your entrance.' I hitched up my skirts and strode into the centre like a man.

'Approach, my Ariel . . . Come!'

I was in my element, aping Mr Kemble's

deep voice as I swept my hand commandingly to my servant, imagining the ranks upon ranks of empty seats before me filled with invisible creatures waiting on my magic. Unlit, the theatre was like a vast echoing cavern, a fitting backdrop to my wizard powers. I could call storms from the ornate ceiling, spirits from under the benches in the Pit, strange music from the silent orchestra.

'Is there more toil?' said Pedro sorrowfully from behind a silver mask. He'd stripped off his street clothes to reveal his costume – vivid blue silk breeches and shirt, topped off with a white cloak fixed to his wrists like a pair of wings. Mrs Reid, the wardrobe mistress, had copied it from pictures of the Venetian Carnival and was very proud of the result. His favourite pearl earring, trophy of his first performance in Drury Lane, hung from his lobe shining dully in the half-light. 'Since thou dost give me pains . . .'

'Louder!' I interrupted, having heard Mr Kemble say it often enough in rehearsals.

'Pretend you're speaking to a hard-of-hearing dwarf in the gods.'

Pedro gave a snort and hitched his voice up a peg for the rest of the speech. Listening to him, I realized that he was showing real promise. I'd seen many actors come and go at Drury Lane, but none had his grace and feeling tone. Not that I was going to tell him, of course: he already had too keen a sense of his own greatness. I wasn't about to sharpen it further.

And now for Ariel's acrobatic exit. Pedro was to tumble off stage in a series of cartwheels, back flips and somersaults. Giving me a cheeky wink, he took a run up and –

Clap, clap, clap.

Pedro crashed to the floor at the side of the stage as a slow round of applause rang out from the shadows of the Pit, startling us both.

'Oh, well done, Pedro, well done.' From the auditorium came a man's voice. He had a strange accent – American or West Indian, I guessed.

Pedro froze. Sprawled in the dust, his dark

eyes looked up at me through the slits of his mask, wide with terror. It was his expression that made me feel afraid. I moved to the edge of the forestage and shaded my eyes from the guttering footlights, my heart beating unsteadily in my chest. Few things could stop Pedro in his tracks but this person had succeeded with no more than the sound of his voice.

'And my, little gal, you ain't bad neither – not that Kemble need worry for his position any time yet.'

A broad-shouldered man in a brown jacket and black breeches was making his way down the central aisle, an iron-tipped cane in his hand. As he approached, he seemed at first glance a handsome man, bronzed by the sun. But when he stepped into the pool of light by the orchestra, I saw his eyes were hard, the lines around his mouth cruel. Black hair shot with grey straggled from beneath his hat. He walked as if he owned the place – it annoyed me intensely.

I bobbed a curtsey. 'I'm sorry, sir, but the theatre's closed until six,' I said tartly, clearly signalling that he was not wanted here, whoever he was.

He waved me away with his cane like a bothersome fly.

'I ain't here for no play. I'm here to reclaim my property.'

Thinking he had probably dropped something in the scrum to get out the night before, I asked more politely than he deserved: 'What have you lost, sir? Perhaps I can fetch it for you?'

He gave a belly laugh. 'Maybe you can, missy. I've come for my slave – Pedro Hawkins.'

I heard a whimper as Pedro scrambled to his feet. Clasping my hands behind me I made rapid 'get going' gestures, giving him the chance to back slang it out of the theatre.

'Your slave? I think you must've made a mistake.'

'I don't make mistakes,' said Hawkins, moving closer. 'He's my boy and I'm coming to get him.'

8

'Is that so, sir? Well, I'm sorry, but you can't have him,' I replied airily.

'Oh, can't I?' With unexpected agility for one so large, the man bounded across the orchestra pit and clambered on to the stage. I retreated a step to prevent him following Pedro into the wings. 'A bantling like you won't stop me getting what's mine,' he added, swiping the cane at me. I tried not to flinch.

'Of course not, sir,' I replied, my tone studiously polite. 'What I'm trying to tell you, sir, is that the Ariel you just saw isn't your boy Pedro.'

'No?' the man said sarcastically. We were now doing a strange sort of Barnaby dance: shuffling to and fro as I blocked his attempts to set off in pursuit.

'No. Sadly, Pedro Hawkins died of a fever last Monday. That was the understudy you saw.'

'Balderdash!'

'It's God's honest truth, sir,' (said with fingers crossed behind back). 'I can understand your confusion – what with the costume and the mask.

But black boys are ten a penny round here. We keep a few in stock in case they up and die in this cold climate as they so often do.'

He wasn't fooled. 'Let me at him then – I'll soon tell you if it's him or no.'

'I can't, sir. I'm not allowed to let anyone backstage. I'll be fined five shillings if I do.'

He felt in his waistcoat pocket and pulled out a handful of coins. 'Here, this'll more than make up for any fine. Now let me by, or I'll stop being so reasonable.'

I ignored the coins. 'I can't do that.'

'Out of my way!' His bloodshot eyes glaring, he raised the cane.

'No!' I stared back at him, my chin thrust forward. I wasn't going to let a big bully like him lay hands on Pedro! The man then lunged, grabbing me by the scruff of the neck. His sudden resort to violence caught me unprepared. I was dangling in his grip like a puppet with broken strings and could do nothing but curse him. How dare he lay hands on me!

'You know what we do with pert gals like you back where I come from?' he hissed, thrusting his cane under my chin. 'We teach 'em a lesson with this.' He jabbed me hard on the jaw. 'That'll stop your mouth.'

'What, sir, are you doing to that child?' a voice roared from off-stage. Mr Kemble strode on to the boards decked out in the crimson robe of the magician, his face made up a startling white with dark eyebrows over flashing black eyes. Power seemed to radiate from him.

'Teaching her some manners,' said the man. He shook me like a terrier with a rat in its mouth.

'He's trying to get backstage, sir! He's trying to steal Ariel!' I squeaked.

'Put her down this instant!' boomed the actor-manager.

'Bring me the boy first.'

'You're talking rubbish, man. Put her down.'

'I told him Pedro died last week but he won't believe me,' I added, half-suffocating under his grip on my neck.

Mr Kemble raised an eyebrow but said nothing to refute the lie.

'Hold your tongue,' snarled the man. 'Don't think for one moment that you can bamboozle Kingston Hawkins, you little witch. The boy is mine by law. You're keeping him here against my will.'

Mr Kemble took a step closer. 'The boy you are talking about is . . . was an apprentice bound to my musical director, Signor Angelini.'

'Your Angelini's a macaroni-eating fool. He wouldn't know a genuine agreement if it bit him on the ass. The man who sold Pedro to him had no darn right to do so. The boy's mine, I tell you, dead or alive, and no jumped-up player can tell me otherwise!'

Jumped-up player! I kicked hard at his shins in my outrage – he had insulted the most admired actor in the land! But in doing so I only earned myself another shake.

'Well, sir, unfortunately for you,' Mr Kemble returned icily, 'you are in the theatre of this "jumped-up player" –' I heard footsteps: Mr Bishop, the irascible stage-manager, ran up brandishing a hammer, his one good eye fixed on my persecutor, the other hidden by his black eye-patch. Behind him, Long Tom appeared out of the shadows slapping a chain threateningly into his palm. '– And you are surrounded by his cast and crew. I suggest you take up your claim with the proper authorities and stop manhandling our Cat as if she were some stray you had a mind to drown.'

My captor let out a hissing breath. Caliban, otherwise known as Mr Baddeley, now stumped into sight, his mass of wild whiskers and mud-splattered sackcloth making an appalling apparition. He was wielding a log with evident intention to apply it to any offending body he could reach. Six extras dressed as sailors followed and formed a semi-circle behind Mr Kemble, pushing up their sleeves in eager anticipation of a brawl.

'You have 'til the count of three. One . . .'

Kingston Hawkins looked around him, counting his opposition.

'Two . . .'

He looked down on my bedraggled head, wondering if I was worth the fuss.

'Three.'

I was dropped to the floor.

'I will be back!' he shouted as he leapt down into the Pit. 'In force. You'd better have my slave or his coffin waiting. And understand this: if he's dead I own even the maggots eating his corpse. You can't keep him from me.'

The door to the Pit slammed. There was complete silence on stage. Mr Kemble extended his hand to help me to my feet.

'Now,' he said lightly as if nothing untoward had happened, 'where were we? Ah, yes: our Ariel has flown off. Hadn't you better bring him back from the dead, Cat?'

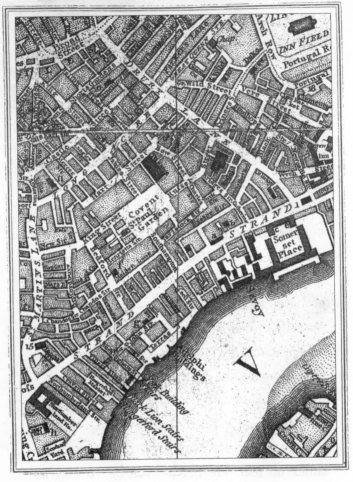

Act I – In which Pedro discovers he
is not without friends and Cat makes
plenty of enemies ...

ACT I

SCENE 1 – PAYING THE PRICE

I found Pedro hiding in one of the practice rooms in the basement, curled up and trembling on an old carpet that had once seen better service as the dying spot. (As you may have noticed if you've been to Drury Lane, actors never die on stage without a rug to stop them spoiling their costumes – this particular one had probably supported the legendary Garrick many years ago.) Pedro scrambled up when he heard my approach. We looked at each other speechless for a moment, the right words difficult to find.

He spoke first. 'Are you all right?'

'Me? Yes, I'm fine.'

'I'm so sorry I ran away.' He was still in a lather of fear. He began walking to and fro, clenching and unclenching his hands. I'd never seen him like this.

'Don't apologise. You did the right thing.'

'Is he gone?' He stopped to look at me. 'Did he hurt you?'

'No, not me.' I surreptitiously shifted my neckerchief to hide my throat.

'I'm so sorry I didn't stay. I should've.' To my horror, Pedro leant against the wall and thumped his head hard, again and again, punishing himself. 'I'm a coward . . . coward . . . coward.'

'Pedro, stop!' I rushed forward and caught him in a tight hug. 'It's all right. Mr Kemble threw him out.' I could feel Pedro quivering. 'That Mr Hawkins thinks you're dead – well, maybe he's only half convinced, but it'll do for now.'

Pulling himself together, Pedro stood up straight, furious with himself. 'I'm sorry. You must think I'm a real girl for behaving like this.'

'Nothing wrong with being a girl,' I said with mock indignation, trying to cheer him up.

'Not a girl like you, anyway,' he replied, smiling despite himself.

I sat down and patted the carpet beside me. 'I think you'd better tell me everything.'

'Where to start?' He held out his hands helplessly.

'Well, for one, I thought you were apprentice to Signor Angelini?'

'I am,' confirmed Pedro, 'well, sort of.' He looked down at his fingernails.

'What do you mean "sort of"?' I sensed he was not being entirely straight.

Pedro sighed. 'I suppose I'm paying the price for it now. You see, my . . . my old master passed me on to a man called Jack Grimes down in Bristol – it was a kind of loan. Grimes dragged me around the provincial theatres and private parties – "the noble savage and his violin", he called me. Dressed me in the most ridiculous outfits.' Pedro curled his lip with distaste.

'Not much changed then,' I said, gesturing to Pedro's Ariel costume.

'If you think this is stupid, you should've seen what I had to wear then. On second thoughts,

I'm pleased you didn't. I feel ashamed just thinking about it.' Pedro managed a wry smile. 'Anyway, last year Grimes ran into Signor Angelini during the summer circuit. The maestro was taken with my talent. Grimes thought he'd make a bit of extra money by arranging the apprenticeship. I knew then that it was an odd agreement – Signor Angelini paid him money to sign me up, realizing he'd get it all back through my earnings. I didn't say anything – the maestro seemed a much better bet than either Grimes or Mr . . . Mr Hawkins. I thought he could teach me things, turn me into a real artist and not just some musical freak show.'

'So Mr Hawkins is right to say that your articles of apprenticeship aren't worth anything?' I asked quietly.

He shrugged. 'I don't know, Cat. Is that what he claimed?'

I nodded.

Pedro stared at the flickering lantern in

misery. There seemed to be nothing more either of us could say.

'I'm not going back to him. I'm not,' he broke out suddenly. 'I'll kill myself before I let him a lay a finger on me again.' Pedro ground his fist into his palm.

'Of course you're not. He can't take you against your will.'

'What? Him a rich man, and me a runaway slave – who'll protect me?'

'Who'll protect you?' I caught his hand in mine. 'Why, your friends of course.'

He squeezed my hand in silent thanks.

'Look, we'd better go and explain all this to Mr Kemble while Mr Sheridan is still out of town.' I rose to shake out my skirts. 'Then I think we should pay a call on Grosvenor Square. I'll send word that we're coming and arrange an escort to keep you safe from that villain Hawkins.'

Pedro's face perked up at this suggestion. 'You think Frank and Lizzie can help?'

'I'm sure of it. It took an earl to get me off a

hanging over the diamond*; a lord and lady might just do the trick for you.'

We were still left with the problem that Pedro was dead.

It was a greater difficulty than you might first imagine. His name was already on all the playbills printed for the opening night of *The Tempest*. Mr Kemble had half-confirmed my wild claim to Hawkins that Pedro had succumbed to a fever; he would be in hot water if he was proved to have lied to the man. It didn't matter what I said – no one took *me* seriously – but Mr Kemble's word counted for something in London. As Pedro and I made our way upstairs, I realized that the first thing we had to do was straighten the matter out.

'Pedro, do you prefer to be dead, or should we drop the story?' I whispered as we waited outside Mr Kemble's office. The dress rehearsal

* See the first volume of my adventures, *The Diamond of Drury Lane*, published by Mr Egmont and available from all good booksellers and circulating libraries.

had been delayed – and, by now, everyone knew why. Two half-dressed ballerinas clucked sympathetically at Pedro as they passed us in the corridor. A stagehand, carrying a model of a sailing ship on the way to the carpenter's workshop, slapped him on the back wordlessly.

'I can't see how we can pretend I'm someone else,' said Pedro, leaning against the wall dejectedly. 'I'm too well known.'

'But with the mask, couldn't we . . . ?'

'No,' he cut in. 'Maybe I'll have to make a run for it, but I'd prefer to stand and fight my corner. I feel better now than I did. Like you said, I've got Frank and Lizzie on my side. Syd and the gang will help too. That counts for something.'

'And me.'

'Yes. And my most important ally – you.'

We exchanged a smile.

'Cat! Pedro! Get yourselves in here now!' bellowed Mr Kemble from within. He didn't sound happy. And who could blame him? He thought he had a box office draw in Pedro; now it seemed he was harbouring an item that could cost him dear. We trooped into the office and found Mr Kemble seated with Signor Angelini.

'Tcha! Tcha!' tutted the musical director, flapping a silk handkerchief at his apprentice. 'Why you no tell me, Pedro?'

Pedro hung his head. 'Sorry, maestro. I didn't realize he'd come after me.'

'It worse than that. He now ask for your earnings over this year. He seek that from me!' Signor Angelini gestured to a letter lying on the desk. 'Immediate return of property, living or deceased – that means you, Pedro – and full reparation! I feel like deceasing you myself! You know how much that will cost me?'

I thought it very unfair to blame Pedro for this. It was hardly his fault that he had been a resounding success. Nor did a few pounds seem anything compared with the prospect that Pedro might end up being handed over to Hawkins.

'You're not going to let him have Pedro back, are you, maestro?' I interrupted him. 'It's not fair. He doesn't want to go.'

'Quiet, Cat,' snapped Mr Kemble. 'Of course we don't want to deliver Pedro up to that man. Slavery is an evil – but it is legal in the British Empire. I'm not sure if we can stop this Hawkins taking Pedro if he is his as he claims.'

I couldn't be silent at this. 'But he's not a dog to be passed from owner to owner. He's a boy – a man like you.'

'You're wrong, Cat,' said Pedro sullenly. 'I'm no more than a dog as far as my old master's concerned. It seems others think the same.' He cast a bitter look at Angelini.

'No, no, boy, it is you that is wrong,' said the Italian, his voice softening. 'I angry with you, *si*, but I do not think of you like this. There is no slavery in music. You have a talent that places you among the great. To me it no matter if you be black, red, green or blue: you play like a god. We try to stop this monster Hawkins. We stand with you.' He patted Pedro on the arm. Pedro made to draw away, but catching sight of the Italian's sincere expression he checked himself, and accepted Angelini's gesture without resistance.

'But how to do it – there's the rub,' murmured Mr Kemble. 'I as good as told Hawkins that you were dead.'

'You didn't, sir,' I butted in. 'That was me. You only said he *had* been the maestro's apprentice. Now you know he isn't.'

'An excellent quibble, Cat. The courts lost a formidable barrister with you being born female, but we all know what impression I allowed Hawkins to form. So, the question is: do we admit you are still alive or do we continue to claim you're mouldering in your grave? I leave the choice to you, Pedro. But I should warn you: if you decide to play dead you'll have to leave us. I can't keep the deception going if you're still here – not even Mr Sheridan can protect you in London, in spite of all his political connections. However, we might be able to do something further afield. I've a brother in Scotland – if I asked, I'm sure he would take you on at his theatre. That might be far enough to escape Hawkins' clutches.'

Pedro looked down at the floor, weighing his options.

Some moments passed and then his mind was made up.

'Thank you, sir, but I prefer to take my chance here. I can't run forever.'

Mr Kemble sighed.

'Good boy,' he said approvingly. 'For what it's worth, I think you've made the right choice. Drury Lane's behind you.' He got to his feet to move to his dressing table. 'You know, I think the best strategy might be to brazen it out in public.' He picked up his make-up stick and began darkening his eyebrows. 'You're a popular performer – the London crowd won't want one of their favourite stars dragged off to waste his talents on a Jamaican sugar plantation. Mr Hawkins may just find that he's taken on more than he bargained for when he came to claim you . . . Off you go now.'

''Ave a care, Pedro,' called Signor Angelini after us. 'Stay with your friends. 'E may think to make snatch of you, willing or no.'

After the rehearsal Pedro and I retired to my home in the Sparrow's Nest – the vast costume store that occupied the attic on one side of the theatre. It was dark up here: the costumes glimmered half-seen in the shadows, like a headless army waiting for the command to march downstairs and on to the stage. I lit a candle. Pedro wasn't called for the performance tonight so he had an evening off duty.

'What a day!' I exclaimed, throwing myself on the old sofa that served as my bed. I saw with a groan that Mrs Reid had left a pile of mending for me with a note complaining about my prolonged absence from her side. Resigned to the inevitable, I picked up my needle and began to work. Pedro barely seemed to notice what I was doing, but stood at the window listening to the hubbub of the audience gathering below as it waited for the doors to open. He stared out over the smoking rooftops at the stars.

'These are the same,' he said, finally breaking the hush that had fallen between us.

I put aside a badly darned stocking and came to stand beside him. The night sky was un-touched by the glitter of lights spilling out from the gin palaces and taverns on the streets below. Up here, at the top of one of the tallest buildings in town, Pedro and I occupied a strange borderland. Look down and you saw Drury Lane spreading her tricks out before you with all the flash showmanship of a pavement magician. London's a city of false prophecies and illusions where the streets are only paved with gold on a wet night with the lamps lit. Look up and all that tawdriness is left behind, for above the rooftops is where the true-silver magic of the starlight takes over.

'What's the same?' I asked softly, caught in the spell with him.

'The stars. They've stayed with me, though

everything else has changed. I remember them shining over my village. My father used to tell me stories about them.'

'What stories?'

'I can't remember. I was too young.' Pedro rarely spoke of his family. He'd lost so much: his home, his family – even his memories.

'You miss them, don't you? Your family, I mean.'

'Every day. My mother's smile. My sisters' bickering – you would've liked them. My grandmother – she wasn't taken – too old, they said. My father – proud and strong. Did I ever tell you he was a king among our people?' I shook my head. 'Funny that Syd's gang call me "Prince" now, isn't it?'

It was a very sad kind of funny, I thought.

'I can also remember the stars at sea. When I got out of the hold of the ship they crammed us aboard, I can remember thinking that the stars were the most beautiful sight I'd ever seen – so high, so free.'

'Was it so very bad in the ship?' I ventured. Pedro had hinted as much before but the events of the day seemed to have unlocked a door to those memories.

'I can't tell you how bad it was, Cat. Not in my own words.' He paused for a moment. 'You know that bit in *The Tempest* where Prospero talks about Ariel being shut in a cloven pine by a witch?' I nodded. 'Every time I hear those words I think of the ship. That's what it was like – a horrible spell. Bodies flung together with no hope of release except death or slavery. We were packed so tight, there was no room to move. The air stank. For months we suffered beyond anything I thought possible. Our people died in their chains, only to be chucked over the side like rubbish. Sometimes the slavers didn't even wait until they were dead.' He leaned his forehead against the glass, shaken by the memory.

I felt sick. 'Pedro, I'm so sorry. It's an outrage that this still happens! I thought we were supposed to be a Christian nation. How can people do this to others?'

Pedro picked up a rich-red velvet robe from the chest under the window and crushed it in his hands. 'I've asked myself that so many times, Cat. I don't have an answer. I thought white people were all like that until I met you.' He looked at me briefly as if to reassure himself that I was still there. 'Now all I can think is that those slave traders are a particularly savage tribe. They don't think of us as human at all. It's as if a skin colour blinds them to everything else.' He turned back to the window. 'You know something? I hope my family is dead.'

'What!'

'Better dead than with a master who can beat you within an inch of your life – demand your every moment be spent dancing attendance on him – kill you if the fancy takes him. Better dead than that.'

'I suppose so.' I had a trembling feeling inside; the depth of Pedro's despair terrified me.

I wanted to pull him out of it. 'But perhaps your family escaped? Or perhaps they found a kind master who set them free?'

'You really think so?' Pedro asked in a hollow voice.

'Well, you don't know for sure, do you?' I continued, despite suspecting that he thought me a fool. 'But you have to imagine something so why not something good?'

'Hah!'

'That's what I do.'

'What *you* do?'

'Yes. In my mind my mother was a beautiful lady and her husband handsome and rich.' As I spoke, the words seemed to make the tale true. I warmed to my theme. 'A wicked nurse stole me in a fit of jealousy and left me on the steps of the theatre, but my parents have never given up hope of finding me again.' My imaginary mother and father hovered in my mind's eye for a moment, smiling.

'You think that, do you?'

'Some of the time. I have other stories too.'

'Do you have one where your mother was a beggar and your father could've been anyone?'

'Pedro!'

'For that's the truth, isn't it, Cat? Just as my family are probably dead or in chains. And the dead ones are the lucky ones.'

'Why did you say that? What harm have my stories done to you?' I asked, unable to swallow a sob.

'Because they've kept you living in a dream, Cat. This place – it's fed you a load of make-believe. Stupid happy-endings.' He grabbed my arm and pulled me close to the window. 'Take a look around you and see what's out there. I live in the real world and I can't afford daydreams. I'm very likely to go back into the service of a violent, evil man. So perhaps even you can understand why I don't want to hear your ridiculous ideas about my family!'

I wrenched my arm from his grip. 'I'm sorry, Pedro,' I said with dignity. 'I was only trying to help. I'll leave you to your stars.' And I picked up my mending and carried it off to the Green Room.

When I came back after the performance I was already regretting that I had left Pedro so abruptly. I would've liked the chance to make it up with him but the Sparrow's Nest was empty. The stars still shone coldly in the night sky but there was no one to look at them.

It wasn't until I turned back the covers on the old sofa I sleep on that I saw that Pedro had left a sprig of lavender on my pillow and a note.

'Sorry, Cat. Sweet dreams,' it said.

SCENE 2 – ABOLITIONISTS

Lady Elizabeth, daughter of the Duke of Avon, poured her guests tea from a silver teapot.

'I can't offer you sugar,' she said as she handed around the china teacups. 'We're no longer taking it.'

'Oh?' I asked, surprised. I knew Lizzie had a liking for sweet things. 'Has the tooth puller warned you off?'

She shook her mass of shining chestnut curls. It never ceased to amaze me how she could always look so perfect – fine white skin, intelligent blue eyes, neat silk skirts. I'd only been in the parlour for two minutes and I was already aware that my ginger ringlets were tumbling from their pins, my 'visiting' muslin dress was as rumpled as if I'd been playing in a haystack and my nails, I noticed now, were distinctly grimy. Syd Fletcher, leader of the Butcher's Boys and our escort for the day, seemed strangled by his collar as he tried to accommodate his six-feet of muscle on a spindly chair that looked in peril of immediate collapse. Only Pedro did the lower classes credit as he sat bolt upright in his spotless blue and yellow livery.

'So why no sugar?' I asked, winking at Syd as he juggled with the tiny cup in his ham-sized fist.

'To support Mr Wilberforce, of course,' said Lizzie, passing a plate of cakes to Frank to hand round. 'Try a piece – the chef's experimenting with honey.'

I have to admit that I didn't know who Mr Wilberforce was – or why he should've taken against sugar. Pedro, however, helped himself to a large slice of fruit cake and took a defiant bite.

'I'm very pleased to hear it,' he said approvingly.

'Sorry, but can someone enlighten me?' I asked.

'Oh, Cat, you know so much about some things and so little about others,' said Frank with a twinkle in his eyes. He'd grown up a lot since I last saw him. Boarding school had stretched him a few inches but not, I was pleased to see, taken away his mischievous grin. 'Mr Wilberforce is trying to pass a law in parliament to end the trade in slaves.'

'That's good,' interjected Syd, taking a mouthful of cake. 'I don't 'old with no slavery.'

'Well said, Syd.' Frank saluted him. 'Then you might be interested to know that Mr Wilberforce's supporters are showing their colours by refusing to buy goods produced by the slave-owners in the West Indies – sugar, cotton and so on.'

I looked down at my clothes. I was decked from head to foot in this very cloth, but then I had nothing else to wear. I took what I got given by the theatre and I doubted Mrs Reid would have much time for the politics of cotton. Noticing my guilty expression, Frank patted my hand.

'I don't think Mr Wilberforce would expect you to go naked for the cause, Cat.'

'Frank!' said Lizzie in a shocked voice. Syd

flushed and gave Frank an angry look.

'In fact, I'm sure Mr W would hate the idea – he's a man of the strictest moral principles,' Frank continued, oblivious to their disapproval.

'You mustn't talk like that to Cat, Frank,' said Lizzie. 'School has made you coarse.'

'So it has, but at least it's not made me a brute like most of my fellow students. Half of them are sons of planters, you know. They'd give me a good pasting if they found out our household was refusing to buy their papas' goods.' He turned back to me. 'Sorry if I offended your delicate ears, Miss Royal. I meant merely to assure you that you did not have to divest yourself of all offending garments before crossing our threshold.'

'I'm most relieved to hear that, Lord Francis,' I replied in kind, then punctured his grand manner with a punch in the ribs.

'Ow! Have you been taking lessons?' Frank nodded at Syd, the local boxing champion, who chuckled, restored to his good humour. 'Now then, my friends – to business. What's caused you to drag me away from a scintillating afternoon of geometry? I had to swear it was at least a family bereavement before they'd release me from that prison they call Westminster School. Great-Aunt Charlotte had to die – again. It had better be worth it. Come on, spit it out.'

Syd put his plate aside. He too had been waiting for our explanation.

Pedro gulped, struggling to find the words. He looked to me for help.

'Pedro's old master, Mr Hawkins, came for him this morning,' I announced.

Lizzie dropped her silver spoon with a clatter.

'Hawkins?' asked Syd. He looked confused. 'Ain't that your moniker? Is 'e your old dad or somethink?'

Pedro shook his head fervently.

'No,' I explained. 'Hawkins chose Pedro's name for him. Pedro was his slave. That vile man bought him during the middle passage to the West Indies. And now he wants him back.'

'Oh, Pedro!' said Lizzie quietly. Frank began walking to and fro in front of the hearth.

Syd turned to Pedro. 'Look, Prince, you ain't without pals now. You're in the gang. No queer cove from foreign parts is goin' to 'urt you. I won't let 'im.'

It was just like Syd to think he could treat the rest of the world as if it were Covent Garden. But I wasn't so sure. There was something about Hawkins that made me think he was more than a match for the Butcher's Boys. Not in a fair fight, of course. Syd could trounce all comers in the boxing ring, no problem, but Hawkins appeared a man of means. He had threatened the law on Mr Kemble. Not even Syd could do anything about that.

Frank stopped his pacing and swung round to face us.

'Well, you've come to the right place. I agree with Syd. No way will we let Hawkins get away with this.'

Lizzie looked up, a hesitant smile on her face.

'Of course, Frank's right. We've got friends among Mr Wilberforce's abolitionists. They'll know what to do. You must leave it with us.'

Suddenly, there was an explosion of yapping at the parlour door and a white lapdog burst into the room. With all the velocity of a small cannonball, the dog leapt into Frank's arms and covered his face with licks.

'Bobo?' exclaimed Lizzie in astonishment. 'But that must mean . . .'

'Mama! You're back!' cried Frank. He dumped the dog on to Syd's lap and ran to the door as a large lady decked out in eye-scorching pink sallied into the room.

'Where are my little chickens? How I have missed you!' she cried in a ringing voice. 'Frankie – how clever of you to be here to greet your old ma! Still giving them hell at school, I hope. How's the Avon rear protector selling?'

'Going like hot cakes, Mama.' He kissed her twice on her rouged cheeks.

'Avon rear protector?' Pedro muttered as Syd

struggled with a dancing armful of fluff. I shrugged, though I could take a shrewd guess as to what it might be protecting the wearer from. The masters at Westminster School were famous for their attachment to the cane.

'And Lizzie! Still here? Not run off after your handsome rebel lord yet?' said the Duchess of Avon, kissing her daughter.

'Not yet, Mama.'

'What's wrong with you, girl? At your age, I would've thrown off the parental shackles and hopped on board the first boat to America to see him.'

'Perhaps I'm rebelling against the parental shackles by not doing as you say, Mama,' said Lizzie with a smile.

'True,' chuckled the duchess. 'Fortunately for us all, Lizzie, you inherited your father's wit rather than mine. No one ever said the Bristol Nightingale had a fine brain. A fine voice, yes – that was what caught your father – as well as a fine –'

' – Mama,' interrupted Lizzie loudly, 'I don't

think you've met our friends. Remember, we told you about them? May I present Miss Royal, Mr Hawkins and Mr Fletcher?'

The duchess now noticed us standing by the tea table. I bobbed a curtsey. Pedro and Syd bowed.

'Who?' she said coldly, lifting a pair of spectacles on a gold chain.

'Cat, Pedro and Syd,' Frank whispered. 'You know – from Drury Lane.'

'Why didn't you say so at once, you ninnies! Thank goodness you're not wasting your time with those stuffy respectable types your father favours. Drury Lane! My, my. I was there when Mr Garrick ruled the roost.' She chucked me under the chin – I couldn't help staring: she had been one of us, a singer, but was now a duchess! 'How's that for a make-believe ending?' I wanted to ask Pedro.

'Oh, yes, I've heard all about you three,' she continued, looking Syd up and down with admiration. 'The conqueror of the Camden Crusher, if I'm not mistaken?' Syd bowed a second time, impeded by his lively burden of yapping dog. 'Come, come, don't stand on ceremony.' The duchess bent towards me. 'Fill me in on all the gossip, my dear. Who's Mr Sheridan's latest conquest? Quite how much does he owe everyone these days?'

I was spared the need to answer by the appearance of a tall gentleman, his white hair brushed forwards on to his forehead. Enter the Duke of Avon.

'My dear, I heard you had arrived,' he said, kissing his wife's hand affectionately.

'Couldn't miss me, could you, not with all the brouhaha I made in the hall?'

'Indeed not. You were never one to make a mean entrance. How was your journey from the country?'

'Roads were frightful. Almost lost the coach in a pothole near Reading. Scared off a couple of highwaymen at Heath Row. That pistol you gave me makes a wonderful bang.'

'I'm so glad you like it, my dear. Now, have

you met our guests?' The duke turned to smile at Pedro, Syd and me.

'Oh yes, the boxer, the African violinist and the little girl you tried to hang?'

'That's the ones.' The duke gave me a rueful look.

'Yes, we've just been introduced. But you interrupted Miss Cat. She was about to serve me up the most delicious feast of gossip.'

'Mama,' said Lizzie, placing a restraining hand on her mother's arm. 'I'm afraid we've got far more serious things to discuss. Pedro needs our help.'

'Oh,' said the duchess, rather downcast. 'In that case, I'll take myself off to my boudoir and repair the damages of the journey. I can be of no assistance to anyone while still carrying half the roads of southern England on my gown.' She cast me a regretful look as she passed.

'Ask me again later, your grace, and I'll tell you all I know,' I said in an undertone. The duchess brightened visibly.

'Wonderful. What a good girl you are! I can see we'll get on splendidly.'

And trailing silk scarves, she flounced from the room, the duke at her side, Bobo barking excitedly at her heels. All the colour in the room seemed to leave with her.

'That, my friends, was our mother,' said Frank, with a broad grin at our astounded faces.

Joseph, my favourite footman from Grosvenor Square, sought me out on Wednesday morning. He found me emptying chamber pots in the privy out the back of the theatre.

'Miss?' he called, standing tall in his impeccable Avon livery and snow-white wig in the middle of the muddy yard.

I ducked my head round the door.

'Hello, Joseph, how are you?' He had proved himself to be a friend during my unfortunate imprisonment for theft earlier in the year, and I was always pleased to see him.

'I am enjoying most excellent health, Miss

Royal,' he said solemnly, bowing to me as if I were the Queen herself and not a skivvy empty-ing piss down the drain. 'And you?'

'Not bad,' I replied, wiping my hands on my apron and coming out of the privy to receive him. 'Do you have a message for me?'

'An invitation.'

'Oh? That sounds even better.'

'If you like that sort of thing, I suppose, miss,' he said with a disdainful sniff. 'Not my idea of a convivial evening.'

'What is it then?'

'One of Lady Elizabeth's gatherings – the serious set.'

'What's that?'

Joseph handed me a card. 'To us below stairs, you, Master Pedro and Mr Fletcher are the jolly set, these are the serious set. Believe me, we prefer your visits. Far less bother.'

I turned over the card and read a note in Lizzie's elegant script:

The next meeting of the Society for the Abolition of the Slave Trade is to be at our house tonight after dinner. Please make sure Pedro comes. L.

'Tell her we'll be there,' I said.

'Certainly, miss.' He bent forward. 'Is it the young master's debut this Friday?'

'Yes, that's right.'

'Good. I've got my tickets,' he said, patting his breast pocket. 'Had a word with Lord Francis and got the evening off. Tell Master Pedro that me and Mary wouldn't miss it for the world.'

'I will,' I promised.

'Splendid.' Joseph stood up straight and resumed his peacock bearing. 'I bid you "Good day", miss.'

Pedro and I turned up in good time at Grosvenor Square and were ushered into the library. As the first to arrive, we decided to amuse ourselves on the sliding stepladder that serviced the top shelves of the well-stocked bookcases. It was one of Frank's favourite games and, as he had once told me, the only reason he ever went into the room.

'What do you think these abolitionists are going to be like?' Pedro asked as he sent me flying to the far end of the room with a shove on the ladder. Clunk! I came to a stop.

'Don't know. Joseph said they were "serious" – whatever that means.'

I slid the ladder back.

'Doesn't sound too bad as long as they're serious about helping me.' Pedro propelled himself across the room. Clunk!

'Back together?' he challenged.

'Yes, why not?'

We climbed on board and both pushed off a bookcase marked 'Philosophy'. The ladder rocketed towards 'Natural Sciences' at the opposite end of the room, the two of us shrieking as we hung on.

At that moment the door opened and a little huddle of ladies all in grey and black entered the room.

'Oh my!' exclaimed one. A second shielded

her eyes against the scene before her. The third gave a scream and retreated into the hall.

Clunk! Pedro leapt from the ladder and bowed to the incomers. I tumbled to the floor.

'Ladies, I am very pleased to make your acquaintance,' he said.

I bobbed a curtsey, struggling to hide my giggles. They looked so shocked to find us playing; it was tempting to offer them a ride.

'Well!' said the tallest of the ladies, proceeding further into the library and taking a seat by the fire. 'I suppose thou must be the little African brother whom Sister Elizabeth told us about.' Her two companions followed meekly and sat either side of her.

'I suppose I am, ma'am,' said Pedro.

The lady now turned to inspect me. 'And, child, who art thou?'

Her antique manner of speaking marked her out as a Quaker. Mrs Reid had told me about them: they were an odd religious group who worshipped by sitting in silence. (Mrs Reid had gone on to add that she wished I would convert as I never gave her a moment's peace.)

'Catherine Royal, ma'am,' I said, having regained my composure. 'From the Theatre Royal, Drury Lane.'

'Ah, the orphan,' said the lady, turning to her companions with a grave nod of her head. 'That explains it. Well, Sister Catherine, Brother Pedro, please join us.' She waved to two footstools near her skirts. 'I am Miss Miller; this is my sister, Miss Prudence Miller.' The second lady bobbed her head. 'And this is my youngest sister, Miss Fortitude Miller.' The third lady gave us a shy nod. 'We are here on behalf of the brethren from Clapham. But we are all brothers and sisters before the Lord, are we not?'

'I . . . er . . . yes, I suppose so,' I agreed, glancing at Pedro to see what he was making of all this.

The door now opened again and let in a gaggle of men and women, most of them dressed in similarly sombre colours. Miss Miller began to introduce everyone, but there was so much brother this and sister that – I couldn't keep up. Lizzie came to our rescue, fluttering into the room in a beautiful blue gown, a tropical bird among the sparrows.

'So sorry to keep you waiting,' she said to her expectant guests. Turning to Pedro and me, she added, 'Sorry, dinner overran as it so often does when Mama's here. She'll be here in a minute. Have you met everyone?'

The visitors seated themselves in a circle, leaving Pedro and me stranded on footstools in the centre. Lizzie took a chair just behind us. Joseph and another footman came in with trays of refreshments. He tipped me a wink as he offered me a cup.

'Thank you all for coming,' said Lizzie, rising to her feet. 'Papa sends his apologies – he has business in the House tonight. He said we should start without him.'

Miss Miller gave an important little cough

and took out a sheaf of paper. 'It falls to me then to read out the minutes of the last meeting for your approval.'

She was halfway through a tedious recital of progress on collecting signatures for petitions when the door was flung open and the duchess glided into the room, resplendent in lemon yellow and diamonds.

'Good evening, everyone,' she boomed, nodding to acknowledge the men, who had risen on her entrance. 'Done the dull stuff yet, eh? Can we hear from the boy now?' She swooped down on me and planted a scented kiss on my cheek. 'I'm especially pleased to see you again, my dear. Don't forget to stay behind to keep me abreast of the gossip from Drury Lane!'

Miss Fortitude Miller gave a little gasp.

'Your grace, we had not quite finished reading through the minutes,' said Miss Miller senior primly.

'Oh, you can cut all that. We all approve them, don't we?' Those present meekly mumbled their agreement. 'Splendid. Then let's hear the boy's story.' She took her place in the armchair that had been reserved for her and looked expectantly at Pedro.

Pedro appealed to Lizzie. 'Story? I didn't know I had to speak. I thought these people were going to help me.'

Lizzie blushed. 'They are, but they want to hear from you first.'

Pedro looked across at me a shade desperately. An intensely private person, I knew he hated talking about his past but there didn't seem anything for it. I gave a tiny shrug. He got up, clasped his hands behind his back, and began to speak, staring into middle distance.

'I was about five years old when my family were sold into slavery – '

'Oh, the poor little lamb!' moaned Miss Prudence Miller, taking out a handkerchief and dabbing her eyes. The gentlemen in the back row were shaking their heads sadly.

Pedro looked confused by this early interruption. He coughed and then continued.

'We were separated before being put on board the ship. I never saw my mother and sisters again.'

'Oh, the fiends!' cried Miss Fortitude Miller. The ladies either side of the duchess murmured their agreement. One had begun to take notes.

A hot flush spread up my face. This was terrible. I knew they meant well, but they were treating Pedro's story like some kind of sentimental novel. Didn't they understand that the boy before them had really lived through all this? I glanced at Lizzie. She looked at me helplessly.

Pedro laboured on. He had just reached the part where Kingston Hawkins spotted his musical talent when the door to the library opened again. Two gentlemen came in. Pedro stopped speaking. The first was a tall man with high, gaunt cheekbones, small shrewd eyes, a long nose and prominent chin. He moved like a daddy-long-legs, all knees and elbows. The second was a real surprise: a stocky, middle-aged African, soberly but smartly dressed. He bore a gold ring on a finger of his right hand. Pedro's eyes were now locked on the African visitor.

'Ladies, gentlemen,' said the gaunt man. 'I apologize for our tardiness.'

'Mr Sharp, Mr Equiano, welcome,' said the duchess. 'Do take a chair. We were just hearing Pedro's story.'

'No doubt it is the same dismal tale that many of our African brothers have to tell,' said Mr Sharp. 'I think we already know the salient points, your grace.'

Mr Equiano took a seat by the duchess and turned to Pedro.

'Come, Pedro, sit by me,' he said in a deep, rich-toned voice. 'I think you've sung for your supper enough times before tonight.'

Pedro smiled with relief and bolted for the chair next to his new champion. Watching Mr Equiano, I leant over to Lizzie.

'Who is he?' I whispered.

'Mr Equiano? He's quite something, isn't he? He was once a slave but he managed to buy his freedom. He's one of the most travelled people I've ever met. You should hear him talk about the icebergs of the Arctic Circle! Now he's settled in London, married an English lady, and devoted himself to freeing his fellow Africans. He assists Mr Sharp – that's the other gentleman over by the fireplace. Mr Sharp's a lawyer – a very brave man: he's rescued other slaves before now.'

Mr Sharp coughed, drawing the meeting to attention.

'We are here to decide what we can do for Pedro,' said Mr Sharp. 'I think most of us know that the law states that no one can be removed from British soil against their will.' Mr Equiano patted Pedro on the shoulder. 'I regret to say, however, it is less clear as to whether the institution of slavery can exist here or no.'

'There is no slavery in Christ!' called out one man from the back.

'Of course, my friend,' continued Mr

Sharp, 'we all agree on that in this room. We believe that the very air of this island is inimical to slavery – one foot on British soil and a slave becomes a free man – but no doubt Mr Hawkins will dispute that.'

'And he'd only be saying what many people think, Granville,' added Mr Equiano with the bitterness of experience.

Mr Sharp nodded an acknowledgement. 'However, I think we have been handed an opportunity. Hawkins' threats against Pedro are just what we need to show the public how cruel and absurd the system of slavery is. We must make Pedro's case famous and bring scorn upon Hawkins for his attempt to take the boy away against his will.'

'Hear, hear, Brother!' trilled Miss Fortitude Miller.

'You are correct as usual, Granville,' said Mr Equiano. 'But how can we do it? It takes days to write pamphlets and get them to the right people. *The Times* or one of the other papers might run a story, if Mr Wilberforce asked them, but we haven't got much time. I expect Hawkins is planning to come down hard and fast.'

The abolitionists sat looking at each other, lost for inspiration. How silly when the answer was staring them in the face! Mr Kemble had seen it at once. I couldn't endure this Quakerish silence any longer.

'I know,' I piped up from my lowly seat on the footstool. Thirty pairs of eyes turned to me.

'Yes, sugar, what do you know?' asked Mr Equiano with a lovely bright smile.

'Pedro's debut as Ariel. The play's a gift – almost every line he has will speak to his case. You can't watch *The Tempest* and not want Ariel to go free: it's bound to bring almost everyone on to Pedro's side.' I stood up, feeling at too much of a disadvantage on the floor. 'All you need do is run off some flyers explaining the threat to him, hand them out to the audience in advance, and the theatre will do the rest. There won't be a man or woman in town who doesn't know

Pedro's story by Saturday morning.'

'What a scandalous idea!' exclaimed Miss Miller. 'The theatre's no place for the boy's case to be heard. It's full of loose women and drunken men!'

I flushed with anger and the duchess bridled. 'Are you, ma'am, inferring that all females who appear on stage are immoral?' she demanded.

Miss Miller realized her error. She was in the home of the singer formerly known as the Bristol Nightingale, now the Duchess of Avon. But the Quaker was evidently a woman of strong opinions and she could not bring herself to back down. 'No offence was meant to present company, but your grace must allow that the theatre is not regarded as entirely above reproach by most people.'

'You mean by silly narrow-minded killjoys like yourself!' boomed the duchess.

'Mother!' implored Lizzie.

'I think Miss Royal's idea is a fine one,' continued the duchess. 'Despite being half your height and a quarter of your age, she's got more sense in her little finger than you have in your entire body. It's not the respectable parsons and their wives we want to persuade, it's Jack and Jill public. They don't read learned tracts, but they sure as eggs are eggs go to the play,' she finished, glaring at Miss Miller as if considering her a new-laid specimen that she was about to scramble.

Hiding a smile, Mr Equiano cleared his throat. The duchess made way for him with a regal nod of her head.

'Though I would not have put the matter quite in the terms your grace employs, I agree that Miss Royal is right. However, we must ensure the crowd takes the matter in the way we wish. It's more than possible that, once Hawkins knows Pedro is to take the stage as advertised, he'll plant his cronies in the audience to protest at the abuse of his so-called "property rights". We must have our people there too.'

'What! Us, go to the theatre!' exclaimed Miss Miller senior. Her sisters looked positively faint at the idea.

'Everyone,' confirmed Mr Equiano, giving me a sly grin. I liked him very much: he clearly had a wicked sense of humour. 'Surely the principle of freedom of the individual outweighs any qualms about the frivolity of the theatre?'

The three Miss Millers exchanged looks, nodded, and gritted their teeth.

'All right,' agreed Miss Miller senior. 'We'll do it – for the cause and for Brother Pedro.'

The duchess gave a snort of derision which Lizzie tried to disguise with a coughing fit of her own. She too was struggling not to laugh.

'Then that's settled,' said Mr Sharp, beaming at us all. 'Equiano and I will see to the flyers and purchase the tickets.' He cracked his knuckles as if readying himself for business.

'You'd better hurry,' I chipped in, 'the performance's bound to sell out.'

He nodded. 'Understood. I'll send someone

for them immediately. Then we'll meet at Drury Lane an hour before the doors open.'

The meeting was declared over and the guests got up to go.

'Oh my!' I heard Miss Prudence exclaiming. 'Whatever will the brethren say when they hear about this?'

'Say?' whispered Miss Miller. 'Why, nothing if thou sayest nothing to them. Remember: silence is golden.'

Her two sisters gravely nodded their heads and scurried out of the door before they found themselves engaged in any further frivolities.

SCENE 3 – A GENTLEMEN'S CLUB

'Cat! Cat! Where are you, you little devil? Always underfoot when least wanted, but never there when I need you!' Mr Salter, the prompt and box office manager, was shouting for me backstage. I was up in the flies with Pedro, inspecting the flying rig for his first entrance that night. All we could see of Mr Salter was the top of his curly white head. I wondered whether to keep quiet and stay hidden. But tempting though it would be to remain in the warm, there was the little matter of earning my keep at the theatre. Mrs Reid had made it clear that morning that darning was not my forte, so errand-running it would have to be.

'Up here, sir!' I called.

Mr Salter turned to stare up at the gantry and bellowed, 'Get down here at the double. I've got a big order of tickets to be delivered for tonight – a gentleman at Brook's is waiting for them.'

I looked across at Pedro. 'Mr Sharp, do you think?'

He nodded. 'Shall I come too?'

I knew he really wanted to see Mr Equiano, his new hero. I couldn't blame him. On the other hand, Pedro had a big night tonight: it probably was not a good idea to have him chasing across town as a messenger, especially not with the fog that had settled since yesterday. The damp would be a disaster for his voice. We also had to consider what might happen if we met any of Hawkins' men out on the streets – there was no time to ask Syd to be our escort.

'Don't you think you'd better stay here in case you're wanted, Pedro? If it is them, I'll ask them to come to the Green Room before the performance.'

'Cat! If you don't get down here now, I'll skin you!' shouted Mr Salter.

'Coming!' I grabbed hold of the nearest rope and slid down it, much to Mr Salter's horror.

'You could have used the stairs, you little

hoyden,' he said, handing me a thick sheaf of tickets. 'Now get yourself off to Brook's, the gentlemen's club in St James. Do you know it?' I nodded. 'Just ask at the door. They're expecting a messenger from Drury Lane. Make sure you get a receipt.'

Outside, the day did not seem to have dawned even though it was near midday. Fog, mixed with the smoke of thousands of coal fires, had brewed a spell for invisibility. Hackney cabs rattled down Drury Lane blind to everything but the feeble will-o'-the-wisp lamps of the carriage in front. Woe betide anyone who dared to cross without taking due care! The jarveys would probably just ride over you in this weather and not worry too much about the bump under their wheels. I stuck to the pavement, weaving my way through the crowds. On the corner of Long Acre, a gaggle of gullible country bumpkins had clustered around a card sharp as he waved a pack of cards under their noses.

'Pick a card, gents – any card,' I heard him intone as I passed. 'And I bet you a shilling I can tell you which one it is.'

'Course you will, Joe,' I called out, then muttered in his ear, 'it's the one you'll palm off on them from up your sleeve.'

Joe 'The Card' Murray grinned and caught my arm. He was one of the less respectable members of Syd's gang. His gold tooth glinted in the light of the shop window behind him.

''Ow's you, Cat? 'Ow's Prince?'

'Bearing up, Joe. Are you coming tonight?'

'Course. Purchased me ticket first I 'eard of it.' He looked at his listeners – their attention was beginning to wander. 'Right, the little lady 'ere is goin' to 'ave first guess. Take a card, miss.' I plucked a card from his hand, seeing if I could spot the exchange, but he was too quick for me. He paused dramatically, hand pressed to his forehead in earnest thought. 'I think it's the ace of spades.'

I turned the card over. It was the four of

diamonds. The bumpkins laughed.

'You owe her a shilling,' one called out.

'That I do.' Joe presented me with a shilling. 'Spend it wisely, little miss. 'Ow about some nice satin ribbons?' He opened his jacket to display a rainbow of ribbons dangling there.

'Not now, Joe, I'm on an errand. See you later.'

Joe turned back to his audience, undaunted by his failure. I knew exactly why he'd done it: if his audience thought they stood a fair chance of winning, they'd be freer with their shillings. His loss to me was a good investment.

I turned south, giving the patch known as the Rookeries a wide berth. My old enemy, Billy Shepherd, had increased his grip on the streets of St Giles since we last met. Rumour had it that he was now the top man in the district, thanks to a few throat-cuttings and arson attacks on those who had held out against him. I would certainly not be welcome if I strayed into his territory. He still had a price on my head following our last encounter in the holding cells of the Bow Street Magistrate's Court.

Now the crooked streets of Covent Garden gave way to the wider carriageways of Piccadilly. The people on the pavements were noticeably smarter. I counted six gold pocket watches in the space of a hundred yards and at least three pickpockets – a sure sign of riches. The shops were also a good deal more flash. James Lock & Co. displayed an array of hats like an aviary of exotic birds. Gray's, the jewellers, tempted the purse with ropes of pearls and trays of gold rings like a pirate's cave.

Finally I reached Brook's, mounted the steps and rang the bell.

'Yes?' a footman challenged me pompously.

'I'm the messenger from Drury Lane,' I said breathlessly.

'They sent a girl – to Brook's?' Incredulity was written all over his face.

'As you can see.' I silently cursed Mr Salter, who no doubt thought it funny to send me here knowing the chance that I'd be refused entry.

'We don't allow females.'

'I know. I don't want to put my foot across your poxy threshold. I just want to deliver my message. You can take it in for me, if you want.'

The footman frowned. 'I can't do that, miss. The member was most insistent that he receive the message in person. There's a receipt to go back.'

I'd forgotten that part. Mr Salter had mentioned something about it.

'Well, you'd better smuggle me in then,' I said, amused by the expression of horror working its way across his face. 'I'll try not to be too obviously female. I'll keep the swoonings to a minimum and promise I'll have only one fit of the vapours.'

The footman curled his lip. 'You – the vapours! Ha! Brats like you can't afford that luxury.' This was very true but need he rub it in? 'Come on then, follow me and keep quiet. I'll take you up by the backstairs.'

Quickly checking that no one was watching,

the flunkey marched me across the black-and-white tiled foyer, through a swing door and into the servants' hall. Ignoring the shocked looks of the off-duty footmen, he led me up to the second floor.

'He's in the billiard room,' the footman explained as we walked quickly along the carpeted hallway to a door at the end of the corridor.

'The messenger from Drury Lane, sir,' he announced, ushering me in.

The first thing I noticed on entering the room was a great expanse of green cloth scattered with shiny balls. The second was Mr Kingston Hawkins crouching over the table at the far side, holding a long cue. He took aim and struck a white ball hard. It collided with a black one and sent it rocketing into the pocket directly in front of me.

'Well, well,' said Hawkins, standing to take a chalk from the edge of the table and rubbing the end of his cue. 'This sure is an unexpected bonus. That, gentlemen, is the little liar I mentioned. You can leave us, Michael. I'll send for you when we've finished our business together.'

'Very good, sir.' The footman bowed.

The door clicked shut behind him. Out of the shadowy fog of tobacco smoke emerged four or five other gentlemen. A second billiard player approached the table, cue in hand.

'Good shot, Hawkins,' he said. 'I see you've not lost your touch while you've been away.'

'Indeed not.' They seemed to be talking about more than just billiards. I stood with bowed head, wondering what would happen next.

'You've brought me the tickets?' Hawkins asked, closing in on me around the table.

'Yes, sir.' I held them out and was cross to see my hand was trembling.

'Good.' His eyes were fixed on my face. He reached out to take the tickets but then, at the last moment, changed direction and seized my hand in his fist. His palm felt strong and hot to the touch. He pulled me towards him, the tickets waving between us like a fan. 'Intriguing, ain't it, gentlemen? She pretended my boy was dead to stop me getting him back. That's theft when you think about it. She's kinda young to be so evil.'

Me – evil! Well, that was rich coming from him. I looked up into his fierce blue eyes and was stunned to see that he really believed what he was saying.

A man stepped into the light from my right. He was in clerical dress and wore a white wig square over a face with a bulbous nose. Taking a monocle from his pocket, he peered at me short-sightedly.

'Interesting, Hawkins, very interesting. It's the riff-raff of her sort that are sapping the very marrow of our empire – attacking property rights like a canker in a once healthy body, undermining our very constitution. Left to run riot, you get the kind of nonsense we see in France – kings humbled, butchers and bakers raised up in their place.'

'Good grief, Dr Juniper!' said the other man with a cue. 'You make her sound very dangerous.

All I see is a scruffy urchin wondering when she's going to get her tip for carrying her message. Hardly a portent of the millennium!'

'Ah, that's where you're wrong, Ferdinand, quite wrong,' said the doctor.

'Yes,' said Mr Hawkins with an exultant smile, 'let's have a better look at the creature.' He let go of my wrist and seized me by the waist. Before I knew it, I was standing on the billiard table directly under the candelabra.

'Mind the cloth!' protested Ferdinand, not at all bothered on my account but staring in concern at my muddy boots.

'Let me down!' I said, adding reluctantly, 'Please!'

'No, no, not until we've finished, missy,' said Hawkins gleefully. 'You see, gentlemen, I'm an expert in judging human specimens. It's my stock-in-trade – I do it all the time in the slave markets. I knew that my boy Pedro was gifted from the angle of his brow. Now, this gal here –'

'Ah! I see it,' said Dr Juniper. 'The red hair

and green eyes of an Irishwoman – an inferior race, as I'm sure we all agree, only one step up from the African and Asiatic savage. And observe her thin, stunted stature.' He took up Mr Hawkins' billiard cue and pointed to me as if in a lecture hall. 'Clearly not strong. I've no doubt she'll end in an early grave.'

'And do you see the shape of her skull?' Mr Hawkins continued. 'I've seen the same on some of my slaves – all of them have been liars with no respect for authority. It's in the space between the eyes – I can always tell. I make sure they're assigned to particularly hard labour to keep them down.'

'Very wise,' nodded the doctor.

'I pity your slaves, you stinking dog turd,' I hissed at Hawkins, unable to stomach any more of this humiliation. 'Let me go.'

Hawkins shook his head and prodded me back into place. 'And then of course there's the limited vocabulary and resort to obscenities – another mark of the dull-witted. But the final proof is in the teeth.' He hooked my upper arm and dragged me towards him. 'You'll get some work from even the meanest specimen if their teeth are good.' The gentlemen laughed and clustered round to take a closer look. One blew a stream of pipe smoke in my face. Hawkins thrust a finger and thumb into my mouth like a horse-dealer inspecting a nag at the fair. I tried to pull away but his other hand was clamped on my neck. 'Hmm. Not bad – I'd buy her if she came up at a bargain price.'

That was the final straw. I bit down on Hawkins' thumb.

'You little witch!' he shouted, pulling his hand away.

'You can stick your tickets up your bum,' I shouted, anger coursing through me as I cast the tickets into the air like confetti. 'And you can shove the receipt where the sun don't shine.'

I ran across the billiard table, kicking balls in all directions, and jumped off the other side. There was a door – I hoped it was my escape route. I threw it open and found myself in a vast library full of men in leather armchairs. The door banged against the wall. The murmur of quiet talk died, replaced by a horrified silence. They were looking at me as if I was something particularly disgusting that the cat had dragged in. Just at that moment, I hated them and everything they represented. 'And to hell with you lot too!' I shouted as I streaked across the polished floor. My heavy boots made an echoing noise as I galloped through, upsetting side tables and decanters in my passage. At the far side, I crashed into a waiter carrying a tray of drinks. Wine glasses exploded all around me as they hit the ground. Past caring, I ran full pelt down the stairs, ducking under arms that reached out to stop me, and burst out of the front door.

'And that,' I heard one crusty member say loudly as I bolted on to the street, 'is exactly why we don't admit females.'

An hour to curtain up. Pedro's chief supporters

were gathered in the Green Room to plan how to distribute our forces for that evening.

'And what did you do then, Cat?' asked Syd, rubbing the back of his neck in bewilderment.

'And then I bit him.'

Pedro whooped and clapped his hands as Joe 'The Card' grinned like a basket of chips. Mr Equiano gave a throaty chuckle. Mr Kemble patted me on the shoulder, trying not to appear too pleased. Lizzie was the only one to look worried.

'I hope you bit him good and hard,' said Frank, leaning over his sister's shoulder.

'I drew blood,' I said with satisfaction. 'He tastes disgusting.'

'That'll teach him,' said the duchess approvingly. She sat back in her chair, breathing in the air with relish. Surrounded by actors in costume, she clearly felt at home.

'What happened next?' asked Lizzie. Her jewelled headdress glowed against her dark hair and I had already noticed a number of admiring glances coming her way from the stage crew. It was rare to see the real thing backstage. Here, we're all paint and paste that doesn't bear too close an inspection; Lizzie's a true beauty in any light.

'I ran for it, telling them . . .' I remembered to whom I was talking. 'Well, telling them what they could do with their tickets. Oh, and I may have said something along the same lines to the members in the library.' My temporary exhilaration drained away as it struck me that I probably hadn't heard the last of my exhibition of female hysteria in Brook's.

'You've certainly put the cat among the pigeons,' said Frank.

The duchess noticed my glum expression. 'Don't fret, Miss Royal – those clubs could do with a kick up the –'

'At least,' interrupted Frank quickly, 'at least we know for certain that Hawkins is going to be here tonight. We'd better continue with our plan. In view of what's just happened, Cat, I suggest you keep a low profile. That leaves the rest of us. We need to put our supporters in every part of the house as we don't know where Hawkins might strike. It's imperative our side drowns his men out. Syd, you take the gods – Joseph will be there to help. Mama and Lady Elizabeth will be in our box, of course. We're expecting Father to join them with some allies from the House of Lords. I'll be in the Pit with Mr Equiano and Mr Sharp. The other members of the Society will be sprinkled about in the gallery.'

'Very good, my lord,' said Mr Equiano with a bow. 'All that remains is for us to wish Pedro "good luck".'

'No, don't do that,' I said quickly. 'Tell him to break a leg.'

'What's that, sugar?'

Mr Equiano may have travelled the world, but he was woefully ignorant about life in the theatre. 'It's bad luck to wish "good luck" back-stage,' I explained. Mr Equiano raised an eyebrow but the duchess nodded vigorously in agreement. 'You have to wish someone to break a leg.'

'How extraordinary! What a barbaric nation you are. Well then, break a leg – both if that's doubly lucky.'

'I'll try my best,' said Pedro. He was beginning to look sick with nerves.

'That's all Drury Lane asks of you,' said Mr Kemble with a reassuring smile as he left the room.

'And I'm sure you will make our people proud, Pedro,' declared Mr Equiano, thumping him on the chest. Pedro looked choked with emotion. For years he'd been starved of a father's love and I could tell he was beginning to look on Mr Equiano as a surrogate – and no bad choice was it too.

Pedro now retired to get in costume. Everyone else got up to take their positions. In the confusion, Lizzie came over to me and touched my arm.

'Cat, you won't get into trouble, will you, for what you did?'

'Probably.' I shrugged.

Lizzie clenched her fists. 'I feel so angry that Hawkins gets away with treating you like that while you're the one who'll be punished.'

'I know. But that's life, isn't it? Never fair.'

'I think you're very brave. It must have been very humiliating to be treated like that.'

'It was. But I tell you what, Lizzie – afterwards, it made me think about all those thousands of people who are poked and prodded by men like Hawkins in the slave markets each day. At least with me it was only a horrid game. Just think what it must be like to be bought by someone like him – what it was like for Pedro and Mr Equiano.'

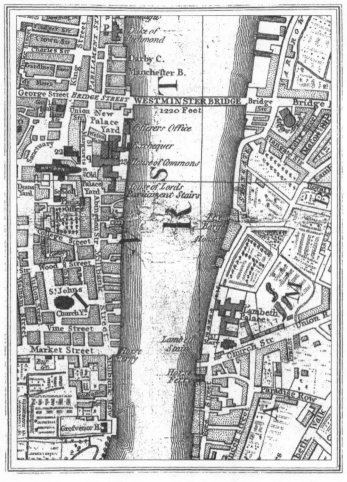

Act II – In which Ariel sweeps all before him . . .

ACT II

SCENE 1 – A TEMPEST

'Here, Cat, have you seen this?' Caleb, the old doorkeeper, thrust a piece of paper in my hand. Outside, a crowd of ticketless onlookers had gathered by the stage door, hoping to catch a glimpse of one of the stars. So far their luck was out as all they could see was Caleb and me. I held the paper up to the light.

Kemble the thief!
Wanted for the theft of one **Pedro Hawkins**, property of Mr Kingston Hawkins. **Britons**, your possessions are no longer safe when men like Kemble are allowed to deprive honest businessmen of their servants. Show your displeasure at this **despicable act** tonight when both the thief and the stolen boy appear on stage together.

*

'We expected something like this,' I said, scrunching up the paper and throwing it in the gutter. 'Did you see our flyer?'

'Aye, that I did. "Don't let the slaver put Ariel in chains! Let the African Ariel go free!" – that's poetry, that is. Better than that muck.' Caleb ground his boot on the discarded paper. 'Saw the slave trade meself when I was a sailor. A foul business, Cat. I'm proud that Drury Lane is backing our Pedro.'

Obeying orders to keep out of sight, I waited until the audience had taken its place and crept into the manager's box, concealing myself behind the curtains. There was a buzz of excitement in the theatre that signalled more than the ordinary interest in a first night. I spotted a number of our friends dotted around the auditorium. Directly opposite me in a box were the three Miss Millers, their hands demurely folded in their laps. I realized that what was normal for me was a big adventure for them.

Joe 'The Card' came in with a party of loudly dressed apprentices from the market and they took positions at the front of the gallery. They seemed to be responsible for most of the paper darts raining down on the Pit as they took the distribution of our leaflet into their own hands. As I watched, the door below the Miss Millers' box opened and Kingston Hawkins entered, his thumb bound in a white bandage. He was accompanied by a large group of men in evening dress. They took places on the benches directly below the Miss Millers, pushing those already seated out of their way. I wondered if our Quaker sisters realized the devil himself had just arrived. Hawkins sat down at his ease and gazed around him. His glance fell on Mr Equiano sitting a few benches in front of him. He gave a contemptuous smile and continued his survey. It was then that I had a feeling that he was looking for me. I ducked back into the shadows, determined not to be seen.

Signor Angelini entered from a side door to

take his place in the orchestra pit. After bowing gracefully to acknowledge the applause, he tapped his baton on the stand. The violins sounded a tremulous note like the hum of the wind in a ship's rigging and the audience settled down for the main business of the evening.

The play opened with a brilliant sound and light show depicting a shipwreck. Reader, if you have not yet witnessed such spectacular effects at Drury Lane, you must purchase a ticket without delay to see the miracle of our modern technology. Mr Kemble had employed an Italian puppeteer to work his magic with a model of a ship foundering in heavy seas. The backstage crew worked wonders with their thunder machine, cranking it for all they were worth. Revolving mirrors were deployed to make flashes of lightning from lanterns hidden in the wings. For extra realism the actors were doused in water as they staggered on stage to deliver their lines, a few droplets reaching the spectators in the stageside boxes near me, causing ripples of consternation among the smartly dressed occupants. The effect was captivating. The audience temporarily forgot the battle for Pedro and was lost in the storm. I saw the three Miss Millers sitting open-mouthed. Miss Prudence was bouncing with excitement in her seat. Even Mr Hawkins had eyes only for the stage, a grudging look of admiration on his face.

But after the next scene change – Prospero's island – the trouble began. Poor Miss Farren, in the character of Miranda, had the first line to deliver. As her stage father, Prospero, played by Mr Kemble, entered from his cave, Hawkins' set started their hissing and booing.

'Thief!' shouted Hawkins.

'Blackguard!' yelled another.

Miss Farren struggled on, but the noise swelled as more pro-slavery supporters joined the barrage of abuse, some throwing orange peel and rotten fruit on to the stage. Miranda is supposed to be in tears during her first speech, but this night they were real. Miss Farren was on the point of giving up when, suddenly, Mr Kemble abandoned his scripted moves and strode to the front of the stage, oblivious to the rain of vegetables. He began to conduct the whistles and jeers as if raising the storm himself. The rest of the audience soon got the joke and a titter of laughter ran through the gallery. Hawkins flushed with anger as Prospero assumed power over the attack upon him.

'Louder!' cried Mr Kemble. 'Blow winds and crack your cheeks!' he extemporized, borrowing from another play.

The crowd cheered and many of us began to howl like hurricane winds, drowning out the feeble cries of the protestors. Miss Farren was completely inaudible but came to the end of her speech with dignity.

'Be collected!' commanded Mr Kemble, returning to script and signalling with a swipe of his hand for the noise to cease. The audience obeyed. Hawkins' crew dared not strike up again: Mr Kemble had humiliated them by demonstrating his power over the majority of the audience. Hawkins resumed his seat, muttering angrily to his companions.

I had thoroughly enjoyed this first battle of wills, but now my heart began to thump as Pedro's entrance approached. What would Hawkins and his gang do then? The moment arrived.

'Approach, my Ariel . . . Come!' Prospero cried.

Starting high up on the right-hand side of the roof, a blue-and-white streak flashed across the stage. It was Pedro, standing on a swing contraption dreamt up by Mr Bishop, to give the impression that our Ariel really could fly. He disappeared from view, then swung back. This time, as the swing reached centre stage, Pedro leapt off and somersaulted to the floor, continuing to tumble and flip until he landed in a bow at Prospero's feet. The audience exploded with excitement at this spectacular entrance. Even Hawkins was driven to give a begrudging round of applause – but then, I suppose he thought all the credit Pedro earned was really his. I could see Pedro crackling with exhilaration as he soaked in the audience's admiration. He delivered his speech with a force that had been lacking in rehearsals. No hard-of-hearing dwarf in the gods would have missed a word.

Trouble only began again when Kemble spoke. 'My brave spirit!' he declared.

'Not yours, Kemble. He's mine!' bellowed Hawkins from the Pit. 'Give him up!'

'Hear, hear!' rumbled the pro-slavery faction from the benches around him.

'Shh!' hissed other members of the audience.

The actors took no notice. Pedro was quivering with excitement like the very spirit of air he was playing. When he came to describing the shipwreck, he was seized by a sudden inspiration and declaimed, 'Hell is empty, and all the devils are here!', pointing with a sweep of his arm at his old master. His wit was greeted with a shout of laughter.

'Too right, Prince!' yelled Syd from the gods.

'Spat out by old Beelzebub 'imself,' bellowed Joe 'The Card' from the gallery where he sat with his feet up on the rail.

Other voices now made themselves heard from all sides.

'You tell 'em!'

'Hands off our Ariel!'

'Leave him alone!'

Things were not going the way Hawkins had anticipated. The crowd loved their Pedro too much. He belonged to them, not to Hawkins. From then on, each speech by Ariel referring to his enslavement to Prospero was met with cheers of support. When Ariel reminded his master of his long-promised liberty, the audience broke into a storm of whistles and catcalls at Prospero's refusal.

'Let him go, you beast!' shrieked Miss Fortitude Miller, waving her fist at Hawkins sitting below her.

'Free him! Free him! Free him!' chanted the young men in the gods. Footman Joseph was conducting the call from the front rail, punching the air with each word.

I don't know how we got through the rest of the play. But seasoned professionals, the actors sailed through their scenes well aware that the real drama was taking place between Ariel and the audience that evening. Pedro was buoyed up by the overwhelming support he was receiving. He flitted about the stage as if on fire with magic, tumbling and spinning, acting and singing like a heaven-sent spirit.

As the play neared its end, I could sense the tension building. We all knew what was to come in the last scene. As the final speech neared, Mr Kemble drew himself up with delighted anticipation. 'My Ariel,' he declared so every man, woman and child in the house could hear, 'to the elements be free, and fare thou well!'

The shout from the crowd was such that I expected the roof to fall in. Heaven knows what those outside thought was happening! Pedro leapt on his swing and was hauled up to the flies, his cloak-wings fluttering behind him.

'Free him! Free him!' thundered the audience.

Hawkins and his crew jeered and whistled, but their protest was lost in the hullabaloo of the crowd backing their boy. With Pedro now gone, the audience turned their attention on his former master. A shout of 'Out! Out! Out!' was now directed at Hawkins. Miss Miller senior leant over the edge of her box and stabbed her finger in the air in time with the chant. Her gesture was taken up by those around her and Hawkins found himself in the middle of a forest of fingers all pointing at him. He got up, raised two fingers to the audience in reply, and pushed his way out of the auditorium. The cheers that greeted his retreat were the loudest yet. My ears were ringing with them long after the epilogue had been delivered by a beaming Mr Kemble.

After the performance, actors, friends and supporters spilled into the Green Room like foam from champagne.

'He daren't touch you now, Pedro!' bubbled

Frank, downing a glass in celebration. 'You're the toast of the town.'

'Yes, you're far too popular now – no one can enslave such talent,' said Mr Kemble, raising a glass to his Ariel.

'You were magnificent!' declared the duchess, planting one of her kisses on Pedro's cheeks and another on a startled Mr Kemble.

'Dost thou know, I think the theatre is quite misunderstood,' gushed Miss Prudence Miller, gazing at the actor-manager with admiration and tweaking her bonnet strings.

Mr Equiano came to stand beside me as we watched the jubilant crowd swirl around our African Ariel.

'Well, you may just have saved him,' he said, nodding at Pedro with a tender expression on his face. 'You should feel proud of yourself.'

I glowed at his praise. 'He saved himself, sir. He faced down Hawkins by his superior talent.'

'True. You both deserve the credit.' Equiano lowered his voice and turned me to look up at him.

'You're closest to him – I can trust you to look out for him, can't I?' I nodded. 'Don't drop your guard yet. Until I see Hawkins sailing away from England, I won't be convinced we've really won.'

'Cat! Cat! Wake up!'

I retired late and had only caught a few hours' sleep when I found myself being shaken awake.

'W-what?'

'Get up, you silly girl. You've got to go.'

I opened my eyes to find myself staring up at Mr Sheridan, my unofficial guardian and the owner of Drury Lane. Back from his visit to the countryside, he was now in the Sparrow's Nest, standing over me with a candle. This was all wrong: he never came up here. Something very serious must have happened.

'Is it Pedro?' I asked, throwing off my blanket.

'No, you fool,' he said tersely. His dark eyes glittered angrily at me. A jolt of fear pushed me to my feet. Mr Sheridan was all that stood between me and destitution: it was by his permission that I found a roof over my head at Drury Lane. If he was furious with me then I was in serious trouble.

'What have I done?'

'You tell me, Cat.' He strode to the window, his back turned. 'I get to my club and find it in an uproar. Apparently some vandal rampaged through the members' library shouting obscenities. How shocking, I thought. Then I find out that the same person had nearly severed a finger belonging to a very respected gentleman. Dreadful, thought I.' He faced me. 'Finally, I'm told it was a girl from Drury Lane and that an official complaint has been made. A warrant is out for her arrest for assault and destruction of property. You can thank your lucky stars that I've arrived before the runners, who, I'm also reliably informed, will be only too delighted to take you into custody. If I didn't owe you one for looking after Johnny, I would have left you to them. What did you think you were doing?'

I stared at him in horror as he said all

this, my mind refusing to take it in.

'It was Pedro's old master, Mr Hawkins. He stuck his fingers in my mouth,' I said in a hollow voice, thinking some kind of explanation was required.

'Cat, you expect me to believe that a grown man put his fingers in the way of your teeth and you just happened to bite down on them?'

'He was pretending to buy me,' I protested, 'like in the slave market. I felt humiliated.'

Mr Sheridan ran his fingers through his hair and swayed slightly. He'd taken in a lot of wine tonight, I could tell, and was perhaps wondering if he'd heard me properly.

'Sounds like he was teasing you, Cat. You shouldn't have let it get so out of hand. But no matter. I can't hide you from the runners – you've got to go, and go now.'

'But where can I go? This is my home!' I whispered faintly.

Somewhere down below, there came a banging on the stage door.

'Open up! Open up!'

'It's them!' hissed Mr Sheridan. 'You're going to have to leave through here.' He gestured to the window. 'They'll be watching the doors.'

I nodded, my brain finally recovering from its bewilderment. I was dressed only in my night-gown. Grabbing a few belongings together in an old sewing bag, I threw the window open, then turned round.

'I'm sorry for the trouble I've caused, sir. Thank you for warning me.'

'Get along with you, Cat,' he said, ruffling my hair in his old affectionate manner. 'You'll be back, I've no doubt. Here!' He thrust some coins into my hand. 'Stay away from the obvious places where they'll look for you – Grosvenor Square, the butcher's shop, and so on. And keep out of any more trouble.'

I nodded and clambered on to the sill as Mr Sheridan closed the window behind me. Clutching my bag under one arm, I scrambled up on to the ridge of the roof and sat astride it. If you edge along the ridge to the gable overlooking Brydges Street, it's possible to slide down to the gutter, swing to the broad window ledge of the tavern next door and then, if you are lucky and the catch is open, climb in on the first floor. At least, that was the theory. I'd never done it before.

With a quick glance back at Mr Sheridan, I began my perilous journey across the tiles. Reaching the Brydges Street end, I leant forward on my stomach to look down to the road. Two men were lounging against the wall opposite the theatre. Moonlight glinted on the buckles of their uniform. Mr Sheridan was right: the runners were after me in force. I would have to make my slide down to the gutter that ran between the theatre and the Players' Tavern as noiselessly as possible. I took a couple of calming breaths. My fingers were frozen – my bare toes also. I had my boots slung by their laces around my neck but dared not pause to put them on. Swinging my leg over the ridge I hung there for a moment, silently counting to three.

'One . . . two . . . three.'

I let go and slid all the way down to the gutter, leaving the skin of my hands and knees behind me on the leads. Thump! I jolted to a halt and gave a hiss of pain.

'What was that?' I heard one of the runners ask on the deserted street below. 'Did you hear something?'

'Nah. Probably just a cat.'

Now for the most difficult part. I would have to come into view – albeit two storeys up – to drop on to the window ledge. I crawled to the edge of the gulley and let myself down, legs dangling over the void. I know it was not the most ladylike behaviour, Reader, but I had no choice.

I must be mad, I thought. Well, it was either break my neck this way or let the hangman do it for me. I let go, dropped to the ledge, and nearly missed my footing. To stop myself falling, I threw myself forward against the sash window; a pane shattered with the impact and glass tinkled to the ground.

A whistle blew on the street below. Not daring to look down, I tugged at the window until it crashed open. I heaved myself in and tumbled to the floor of a bedroom. In the gloom, a man in a nightcap sat up in bed.

'What the . . .!' he exclaimed.

'Sorry!' I hissed as I darted for the door. 'Must go!'

I made my way to the stairs, and there bumped into the innkeeper, Mr Mizzle, on his way down to answer the hammering at the door.

'Mr Mizzle, it's me, Cat. The traps are after me! Don't let them in yet.'

Us theatre folks stick together. As chief provider of ale to the thirsty crew from next door, Mr Mizzle knew that now was no time for the whys and wherefores of the matter. Now was the time to help me escape.

'Out the back, Cat. You know the way,' he said, thrusting me through the kitchen door into the yard. 'I'll keep them busy in here.'

I dashed across the yard, climbed on some

empty barrels and over the wall, dropping to the ground in the alleyway. I then breathed a sigh of relief. From here on, I was safe. I knew the back alleys around Drury Lane better than any Bow Street runner. Hopping into my boots, I threaded my way down to the Strand and ran westwards into the night.

SCENE 2 – SWITCHED

I only stopped running when I reached Westminster Bridge. Panting so hard I thought my
ribs would crack, I leant against the parapet. It
was cold – so cold. As the heat of my dash across
town faded, the frosty air began to bite. I was
shivering uncontrollably. I couldn't remember
ever being this frozen. But then, I'd never been
homeless dressed only in a nightgown, shawl and
boots since – well, since I was a baby left on the
doorstep of Drury Lane. And there was no going
back to the theatre tonight – or for many nights
– perhaps forever.

I stared out at the dark water of the Thames
rolling below, wisps of mist creeping along the
banks. Dawn was breaking and the streets were
coming alive. A barge sailed beneath me, coals in
a brazier glowing as the bargemen warmed their
hands. They laughed gently and took a swig from
steaming cans of tea. The contrast between my

own situation and their cheerful life made the view the most depressing one I'd ever seen.

That's enough, Cat, I told myself fiercely. This is no time for self-pity. You're in a spot of trouble? Well, it's not the first time. You're cold? So you need warmth. That means clothes and a fire – possibly breakfast too if you're lucky.

I pulled open the bundle of clothes I had grabbed in my hurry to escape and found that I'd picked up the breeches, jacket and cap that I'd put by for jaunts out with Syd's gang when I dressed as a boy. Oh brilliant, I groaned. I didn't even have a full set of proper clothes.

But then I had an idea . . .

'You've a message for Lord Francis?' The porter at Westminster School peered at me sceptically from the warmth of his lodge. 'Bit early isn't it?'

'Ain't it just, gov,' I said, legs astride and wiping my nose on the back of my hand in my best messenger-boy manner. 'That's wot I said when the duchess 'erself sent me 'ere.'

'Hmm. Hand your note over and I'll see it delivered when his lordship rises.'

'Well, that puts me in a fair pickle, gov. I's 'avin' the message in my canister if you foller me.' I tapped my cap to indicate my head.

'All right, all right,' said the porter, already tiring of talking. 'Lord Francis has the top room in that staircase by the clock tower.'

I touched my cap and bolted across the courtyard. First barrier overcome; breakfast a couple of steps nearer. As I entered the staircase, I met a young man with curly black hair on his way down.

'Here, tiddler, where do you think you are going?' he said, grabbing me by the arm.

'Message for Lord Francis, sir,' I said, keeping my head lowered. I realized with a horrid jolt that I knew him: it was Frank's friend, the Honorable Charles Hengrave. I'd even read some of my work to him earlier that year at one of Lizzie's tea parties.

He laughed. 'He won't be out of bed until the

bell – dead to the world until the last moment. You'd better leave him be.'

'I can't do that, sir,' I said desperately, trying to worm my way past him. 'It's urgent. It's his Great-Aunt Charlotte. She's on 'er last legs.'

The Honorable Charles pulled me up short by the back of my jacket.

'What? I know for a fact that he doesn't have a Great-Aunt Charlotte.' He turned me roughly to face him – and then let go as if I'd burnt him. 'Miss Royal! I do apologize, but what on earth . . .!'

I made frantic shushing noises. The porter was peering out of his cabin at the altercation going on across the quad. 'Please don't give me away. I'm in enough trouble as it is. I've got to see Frank.'

Charles turned on his heel. 'Come on then. We'd better hurry. Everyone will be up in a moment.'

I followed him up the narrow stone staircase to the very top and he hammered on the door.

'Frank! Frank! Make yourself decent. You've got a visitor.'

Waiting a few moments, my escort opened the door.

'Lucky for you we share a set of rooms,' he said. 'You can't imagine how much trouble he'd be in if anyone else caught him with a . . . well, with a you-know-what in his room unchaperoned.'

We entered the study to find a bleary-eyed Frank standing in a rumpled shirt.

'Who is it, Charlie?'

There were footsteps outside. The porter appeared at the door. 'Everything all right, sir?'

'Yes, Mr Jennings, everything is perfectly in order,' said Charles, shoving me out of sight behind him. 'I was just telling his lordship about the messenger.'

'It's only that I thought I saw the little urchin giving you cheek down in the quad.'

'No, no, he's been very respectful. We were having a joke, that's all.'

'Well, in that case, I'll get on with my work.'

'Yes, yes, you do that. Very good, very good.'

Charles backed the porter out of the door and shut it behind him with a sigh of relief.

'What's going on, Charlie?' asked Frank, still not fully awake. He yawned, stretched and scratched the back of his head. 'What's the messenger here for?'

Charles waited until the footsteps had died away. 'You'd better ask yourself. I must say I'm also rather intrigued to know the answer.'

Frank took his first proper look at me and swore. 'Damn and blast, Cat, what are you doing here?' He grabbed a dressing gown and hastily wrapped himself up in it.

'I was rather hoping you'd let me warm up and have some breakfast,' I replied with a longing look at the fire. 'I've just spent the night on the tiles.'

'Good lord, Cat, you look frozen.' He grabbed my hands, now noticing that they were blue with cold, and rubbed them briskly in his palms, all trace of sleepiness vanished. 'Charlie, get the blanket off my bed.'

Bundled up by the fire, warming up at last, I began to tell them the tale of my escape across the rooftops.

'Miss Royal, you are certainly a most extraordinary young lady!' exclaimed Charles when I'd finished.

'You'd better drop the Miss Royal, sir,' I said. 'I'm a boy for the moment.'

'In that case, you'd better call me Charlie. Can't have you calling me "sir" the whole time.'

'But what are we going to do about you, Cat?' said Frank, striding up and down the hearthrug. 'You can't stay here, you know.'

I nodded. I had known that I couldn't hide out at Westminster School for long but the thought of wandering the streets again was terrifying.

'We've got lessons this morning,' continued Frank. 'Dame Clough, our house matron, will be coming in and out to clean. And Charlie's brother is expected any moment.'

'No need to worry about Tom. I've had word

that he won't be here till after Christmas now. Still not got over his bout of measles,' said Charlie. He then turned to look at me, the flicker of an idea dawning in his eyes. 'No, it wouldn't work. I'm being foolish . . .'

Frank caught the tail end of the scheme before it was completely abandoned by Charlie. 'I don't know.' He put the cap back on my head, inspecting me closely. 'If she's put in the College Dormitory we'd be stuffed, but we could say your mother wants him to sleep in the same house as you because of his delicate health. He could have your room – we could share mine. No one's met him yet, I assume?'

'No. Tom's been with a tutor in Dublin for the past two years.'

'Well, it's possible we'd get away with it then.'

I looked from one to the other, hardly believing they were suggesting what I thought they were suggesting.

'She – he'd have to arrive properly – in a carriage and with luggage and so on,' said Charlie.

'I can fix that,' said Frank.

'You're both mad,' I said. 'I'd be found out in one second flat.'

They grinned at each other.

'Oh, I don't know. You underestimate your acting powers, Cat,' said Frank. 'I've seen you with Syd and the boys. It'd be fun to try, wouldn't it?'

'But . . .'

'And I can't turn you out, can I? Where would you go? You know better than me what can happen to girls on the streets. And you're far more likely to get picked up by the runners if you're out there. The worse that would happen to you here is that you'd be expelled.'

'And you two as well!'

Charlie shrugged. 'I don't mind. I don't like it here that much, to tell you the truth. All they seem to teach is how to bully and be bullied.'

'And you know I never wanted to come in the first place,' added Frank. 'Mama won't mind if I'm chucked out. Father would shout, but not for too long – not when he knows that I did it to help you. So you see, you'd be doing us a favour.'

'You are both mad,' I repeated, shaking my head. 'Cracked. Addled. Raving. And, anyway, what happens when the real boy arrives?'

'That's weeks off yet. It seems to me that the most immediate problem is saving you from the runners.' Frank whisked the cap off my head, letting my hair tumble out. 'Sadly, I think we'll have to sacrifice this to the cause.'

'Yes, Tom Cats don't sport ringlets,' agreed Charlie.

'Shall you be the barber or shall I?'

'I'll do it,' said Charlie, taking out a pair of scissors from his desk drawer. 'She doesn't know me so well yet and is not likely to curse me so loudly when she sees what I've done.'

'You're not . . .' I stammered.

'We are.' Frank suddenly looked serious. 'Unless you have a better idea?' I thought for a moment then shook my head. 'Please, Cat, for my sake – and for Lizzie. I don't want to visit you next at Newgate. I don't make a very good prison visitor – I'm terrible at small talk.'

I bit my lip. What could I do, Reader? On the one hand, I could take my chances on the streets and probably end up in a cell by the evening. On the other, I could try this madcap idea which might, just might, succeed. What did I have to lose?

'All right,' I sighed. 'You can cut it off.'

'To be safe, I think we'd better cut it pretty hard,' said Frank, taking a strand in his fingers. 'You see, you don't look much like a boy, Cat, even with a cap on. What's your brother like, Charlie?'

'Big – makings of a prizefighter.'

'Hmm. Well, the measles have taken it out of him, that's all I can say. Your new brother Tom will be more in the angelic chorister mould.'

I closed my eyes and tried not to think about how long it would take to grow back as the hair dropped into my lap. When Charlie finally told me to look in the mirror, I saw a tousle-haired waif staring back. Cat Royal seemed to have vanished. There wasn't much of me at the best of times – but without my curls I was almost invisible – reduced to a pair of large, tear-filled green eyes in a pale, freckled face.

The boys looked at each other nervously. 'What do you think?' Charlie asked, turning to Frank.

'Not sure. Still too damned pretty.' They were both watching me, worried how I was going to react.

Now my hair was gone, it was too late to back out. I mentally shook myself. There I was, wallowing in self-pity again when they were trying their best to help me. I had to make more of an effort.

'Look!' I said, throwing off the blanket and displaying my scraped elbows and hands. 'My knees are the same. Is that more boyish for you?' I turned back to the mirror, ruffled my hair so that it stuck up at the front and stuck out my tongue at the reflection. 'Thomas Hengrave, pleased to meet you.'

Charlie laughed, his relief palpable. He

strode over and shook my hand. 'Pleased to meet you too, little brother. Now, let's get you some decent clothes and set this charade rolling.'

'So, you have just recovered from the measles, Hengrave, is that so?' said Dr Vincent, the headmaster, looking up from a letter reputing to be from Lady Hengrave. Frank had turned out to be a fair hand at forgery – something Joe 'The Card' had taught him over the Easter holidays.

'Yes, sir,' I said, standing with my hands clasped behind my back, my eyes on the wall behind him. I could sense Charlie shifting nervously by the door, ready to make a bolt for it if the ruse failed.

'And your mother wants you to stay with your brother?'

'Yes, sir.'

'Hmm. Well, I must say you do look a bit sickly. I understood from Lord Hengrave that you were a strong boy with a taste for sports.'

'He is, sir,' said Charlie quickly. 'He's stronger than he looks.'

'We'll see, we'll see. It's most irregular not to have a boy in the College Dormitory in his first year. I always think it's better for all concerned that the house dame keeps an eye on the young ones.'

'I'll keep an eye on him, sir,' said Charlie.

'That's what I'm afraid of, Hengrave. You share a set with Avon, don't you?'

'Yes, sir. Avon's offered to be my brother's substance.' (Charlie had explained to me that every new boy, or 'shadow', had to have a 'substance', or older boy, to sponsor him.)

'Not ideal, not ideal at all. You both have a talent for mischief. I wouldn't want your younger brother to come under bad influences in his first term.'

'We promise to behave, sir.'

'I'll be watching you very closely to see that you do. Hurry along then. Show your brother where he's to go. You've missed enough lessons this morning as it is.'

'Yes, sir.'

Charlie towed me outside to where an anxious Frank was waiting.

'Well?' he asked.

'He bought it. Tom Cat's in. We're to take him to his form immediately.'

Frank seized my other elbow and they marched me briskly across the quad. The bells of Westminster Abbey began to strike the hour – eleven o'clock. In the space of five hours I had become a boy, been dressed in Frank's old clothes, smuggled out, arrived back aboard a carriage loaned from the Avon stables and now enrolled in the Lower Form as the Honorable Thomas Hengrave. And all because I had told some old farts to go to hell.

'You're doing well,' whispered Charlie in my ear. 'Just remember not to twiddle your hair.'

'Sorry.'

'And don't cross your ankles,' added Frank.

'Sorry.' Was there anything else I had to remember?

'How's your Latin?' asked Charlie.

'Non-existent.'

'Well, you might find the next class a bit tough then. Mama will dismiss the tutor when she hears how poorly he's prepared you for school.'

'I want to go home,' I moaned as they pulled me through a high arched doorway.

'No you don't. Even Latin is better than a lock-up,' said Frank cheerfully.

'Just don't do anything to earn the cane, will you, Cat? I'm not sure our plot would survive that,' Charlie said with a frown.

'Sit quiet, try hard, and you've nothing to fear. We'll see you after lessons,' Frank concluded. 'Oh, and give this to the usher – it's his fee.' He pressed a guinea into my hand and pushed me through a door.

It opened on to a vaulted room full of boys sitting in rows, heads bent over slates. They looked up on our entrance. I gulped.

'Yes?' enquired the master, a young, tired-looking man with straw-coloured hair, dressed in a long black gown.

'Mr Castleton, my brother Thomas has arrived at last,' said Charlie, pushing me forward.

'The younger Hengrave? Ah yes, we've been expecting you since September. Quite recovered now from your indisposition?' I nodded and handed him the guinea as prompted by Frank. 'Good, good. You can sit next to Ingels at the front here until we know where to put you in the class ranking.' He pointed to a space beside a fat boy with dull eyes. I sat down, crossed my ankles and quickly uncrossed them again. Charlie and Frank gave me a last look and ducked out of the room. 'We're translating a passage from Horace as you can see, Hengrave.'

I looked up. On the blackboard was a verse – I could tell that from the arrangement – but I could not read a single word.

'Carry on, Richmond.'

A small boy with dark hair and olive skin began to drone on, turning this impenetrable stuff into something resembling English. He stumbled over a word.

'Come on, Richmond, you should know that one. *Amor* – we did the declension last week. Surely even you remember that?'

'Er . . . hope?' guessed the boy vaguely.

'Ingels?'

My neighbour shuffled. 'Cheese?' he tried. A ripple of laughter passed across the room. I couldn't help joining in.

'Cheese? Cheese!' cried the master in despair. 'Your thoughts are on your dinner, not your lesson, Ingels. I despair of you. What about you, Hengrave? Save me from these imbeciles.'

My laughter died. All eyes turned to me. I wondered if they'd noticed that there was something very odd about their new classmate. It seemed all too obvious to me. I felt as if I had a big arrow suspended over my head emblazoned 'Girl!'

'Boy, I asked you a question.' Mr Castleton picked up a thin cane on his desk and began to swish it against his leg.

Reminded of Charlie's warning about beatings, I wrestled my mind round to the problem before me. *Amor, amor.* I knew a French word very like that.

'Love?' I hazarded.

'Exactly.' He tapped the board with his cane. '*Amor* means love. Thank goodness someone has something between their ears. Carry on, Richmond.'

My luck was holding. My complete ignorance of Latin had been hidden for one lesson. If Charlie and Frank gave me some intensive tutoring, I began to hope that I might just be able to fool my teachers for a week or two.

The class was dismissed at midday. As the Abbey bells tolled the hour, I followed the boys outside into the green space of the Dean's Yard, wondering where I was to go next.

'Love? Love? What sort of nan boy would know that kind of stuff?' someone sneered as I passed two boys slouching in the winter sunshine. It was Richmond with Ingels beside him.

I walked on, trying to remember to stride rather than take small steps as I usually did in skirts.

'He looks like a nan boy, doesn't he, Ingels?'

'Yeah, just like a girl.'

It was no good. I'd have to stop or they'd next be shouting 'girl' – and that was an idea I did not want planted in anyone's head.

'Who are you calling a nan boy?' I challenged, clenching my fists.

'Pretty boy getting in a temper, is he?' said Richmond, squaring up to me. 'New boy not know his place? Still, they're all nan boys in Dame Clough's – not like us in Ottley's.'

It seemed he was talking about some Westminster boy rivalry between the boarding houses. I had no idea what a real boy would do in this situation. I had to guess.

'Call me that again and I'll thrash you,' I said, raising my fists in a boxing stance as I'd seen boys do.

'I'd like to see you try,' laughed Richmond, adding, 'nan boy.'

That was it. I had no choice, Reader. I thumped him as hard as I could, remembering to follow through with a hook from my left as Syd had taught me. Richmond went down, but I then found Ingels jumping me from behind. I hadn't planned on that. I went down with him and we all ended up in a confused scrap on the ground, with me taking an elbow in the eye.

'Leave him alone!' Someone yanked Ingels off me. 'Are you all right, Ca . . . Tom?' I was pulled to my feet and saw Frank and Charlie standing beside me, glaring furiously. Charlie sent Richmond packing with a kick up the backside. 'Lay off my brother, Richmond, or you'll be sorry. And you, Fatty!'

'He started it!' moaned Richmond as he limped away. Charlie and Frank looked at me in surprise.

'Damn it, Cat, your nose is bleeding – and your eye!' hissed Frank, tucking me under his arm. 'I told you not to get into trouble!'

'But they called me a girl!' I protested. 'And

insulted Clough's! I thought that's what a boy would do.'

Frank exchanged looks with Charlie. 'They would,' he admitted reluctantly. 'But you . . . you shouldn't. It's not right.'

'Look, you got me into this. I'm just trying to play my part right! Bit late for qualms about seeing me in a scrap, isn't it?' I dabbed my nose: I was dripping blood on to my lip. 'I thought I did quite well considering it was two against one.'

'You did, little brother, I'm proud of you,' said Charlie, slapping me on the back. 'We'll tell the boys in the house how you took on two bruisers from Ottley's on your first day: it'll do your reputation no end of good.'

I gave him a bloody smile.

'Let's get you cleaned up,' sighed Frank. 'I can see we've a long day ahead of us.'

I soon discovered that life as a schoolboy was far more of a grind than I had imagined. When lessons were over, we had a breather for dinner, but then were expected to go to work again at something called Prep.

'What's that?' I whispered as we made our way back into the classroom.

'Preparation for lessons,' said Frank. 'Here – take this.' And he thrust a Latin Primer into my hand. 'I hope you're a fast study. I had a word with Rookie and you're doing Horace again on Monday. Look at Chapter Three.'

'Rookie?'

'Mr Castleton,' explained Charlie. 'You have to watch him, Cat: he's completely obsessed with the Latin play. He'll have you on the stage before you know it. Last year I got landed with a main part.'

'Clytemnestra,' snorted Frank. 'Dress, wig – the works. It was a sight for sore eyes.'

'Yes, well, thank you, Frank, for mentioning that,' growled Charlie. 'I had hoped I'd lived it down by now.'

'You know I'll never let you forget,' grinned Frank. He turned back to me. 'You'll be all right in Arithmetic and Greek – they won't expect you to know much – so I'd concentrate on the Latin if I were you.'

'When this is all over, at least I'll be qualified as a governess,' I groaned, flipping over the cramped pages of text.

'Disqualified,' quipped Frank. 'Girls don't learn Latin, lucky beggars.'

'Shh!' Charlie hissed as Richmond took a seat along the table from us, eyeing my companions resentfully.

Dr Vincent came in and everyone but me immediately got to their feet. Frank kicked me and I leapt up.

'I'm a boy, I'm a boy,' I chanted to myself under my breath. 'Boys get up when elders enter the room.' I let my eyes wander round the room, searching for character notes. I'd never paid so much attention before. Ugh! Boys pick their nose. Boys scratch their armpits. I began to scratch mine, surprised to find how satisfying it was.

'Hengrave Junior, stop that disgusting habit!

We are a school for young gentlemen, not Covent Garden costermongers!' barked Dr Vincent. Frank turned to look at me in astonishment. I winked and linked my hands behind my back.

'You may sit down!'

With a noise like thunder, we resumed our seats and applied ourselves to work.

And that was when a miracle happened. Do you know, Reader, I found that those close-printed pages held a feast of poetry I had never before tasted. I couldn't confine myself to Chapter Three. I had to leaf through to glance at the verses and their translations. Latin was a lovely language, I realized as I sounded out the lines in my head. Why had I not known this? Every schoolboy I met had complained about the tedium of studying it, but why? There was so much here I recognized. Playwrights had mined this stuff for some of the best speeches in English drama. I felt as if I had come home.

The hour for Prep passed in a blink of an eye

and then we were released for what remained of the day. Frank linked arms with me and we went outside. He kept looking at me out of the corner of his eye and shaking his head.

'What's the matter?' I asked as we made our way up into his set.

'It's uncanny. I keep forgetting who you really are.'

'I know. You'd never've gone through a door first when I was . . . well, before today.'

'Did I? Oh, sorry.'

'Don't be sorry. That's just how it should be.'

We arrived back at the set to find Charlie was toasting some bread for supper. The smell was delicious. He buttered a slice for me.

'Ladies first,' he said, chucking it in my direction.

'Don't. I was telling Frank, you've both got to forget all that. Something might slip out by mistake.'

'You're right.' Charlie sat back on his haunches. 'So half-starved Tom Cat's first then.

— 130 —

You look to me as if you've missed a few too many meals, brother.'

I didn't know where to look. His observation was true but I wasn't used to young gentlemen making personal remarks about my appearance. By changing clothes, I'd crossed a boundary and would have to become accustomed to being treated as an equal. Well, I'd better do the thing properly. I slumped in an old armchair with feet up on the fender and took a big bite. You know, girls, being a boy's not half bad. You get to slouch around in comfortable clothes. No one tells you to sit up straight and act like a lady. There were compensations in this otherwise disastrous situation.

'I think we'd better get a message to Syd and Pedro,' I said when we'd demolished a stack of toast. 'If I know Syd, he'll be combing the streets for me. And Pedro will worry.' It now came back to me that I had promised Mr Equiano to keep an eye on my friend. In the adventures of the day, I'd temporarily forgotten the peril he was facing.

Hawkins had effectively rendered me useless by forcing me to go on the run. 'And we'll need to check Pedro's safe.'

'I'd given that some thought too. I sent Lizzie a note with the carriage this morning,' said Frank. 'And I forgot to mention that I got one back telling me on no account to proceed with the plan for you. Too late, hey?' He grinned and chucked Lizzie's note into the fire. 'Syd's easy. We already have an arrangement for passing messages.'

'What's that?'

'I order sausages.'

'Or chops,' added Charlie.

'Sometimes kidneys. The last lot went down a treat devilled for breakfast. Syd or one of the boys brings them. It's getting late, but I'm sure he'll make a special delivery for us.'

Frank disappeared downstairs to dispatch a messenger and I found myself alone with Charlie for the first time. It felt very awkward without Frank. I was suddenly very conscious that I was masquerading as a boy in a strange place with someone I hardly knew. I couldn't stop it – a blush crept up my cheeks. I sat up straight and crossed my ankles.

'You must think me very shocking, getting into trouble with the runners and the rest.'

Charlie stirred the fire. 'Well, I must say you're not a bit like my sister. Not that that's a bad thing,' he added hurriedly. 'She's very much a busybody – a great friend of Frank's sister.' He dropped the poker. 'I hope she doesn't take it into her head to visit me. She's in London at the moment . . .'

'This isn't going to last, is it?' I said, resigned to what I saw as the inevitable moment of revelation. 'I'll have to think what I'll do when I'm found out. I don't want them adding "impersonating a Westminster schoolboy" to the other charges.'

'We'll get you out, don't worry,' said Charlie. 'I won't let my little brother down.'

Syd's arrival was signalled by a loud thumping on the door. Frank opened it and was almost knocked down in the rush of Syd unburdening himself.

'Cat's gone missin'.' He thrust a packet of sausages into Frank's arms. Syd's cheeks were flushed, his eyes anxious. 'The runners are after 'er. They're watchin' the shop – your place – the theatre – the 'ole bloody town. Word is Pedro's old master is payin' them well – and they've a score to settle with Cat, they say.' He gave a distracted nod to Charlie, not noticing me by the fireside. 'I've been lookin' everywhere for 'er – all me boys are out – but she's vanished. I'm that worried about 'er. What if someone got 'old of 'er last night? She's only a little thing – can't defend 'erself. If she spends another night out on the streets, I don't know what I'll do.'

'Do, you great lump?' I said, tears in my eyes at hearing his concern for me. 'You'll stop worrying yourself to death this instant, that's what you'll do.'

Syd did a double-take. 'Cat? Cat! What the 'ell 'ave you done to yourself?' He folded me in a rib-cracking hug and then pushed me to arm's length to take in my transformation. 'What you done with your 'air?'

'Charlie cut it off.'

''E did what?'

Charlie took the sensible precaution of backing out of Syd's reach behind an armchair.

'I'm his little brother,' I said, bowing. 'Tom Hengrave. Can I join the gang now?'

'No, you bleedin' well can't, Cat Royal! 'Ave you gone mad or somethink?'

'Think about it, Syd.' I was trying to be reasonable for the both of us but Syd looked more wild-eyed than ever. 'It's all for the best really. You can't hide me – neither can the theatre. I had to go somewhere and here's where I ended up. No one's looking for Tom. They all think Cat's on the street somewhere – and that's where I'd be if it weren't for Frank and Charlie.'

'It won't work,' declared Syd. 'You don't know 'ow rough boys can be, Cat. What if one of them sets about you, eh?'

'They did,' said Frank cheerfully, putting a frying pan on the grate and filling it with sausages. 'Two of them. But Tom Cat sorted them out, didn't you?'

I nodded. 'Though I could do with a few tips from the master. I've learned that, apart from Latin, the boys here do little else but fight.' I looked up at Syd and pummelled his stomach playfully.

He frowned and shook me off. 'But they'll notice soon enough.'

'Notice what?' asked Charlie innocently.

'Well, that he's a . . . he's a she,' Syd said delicately.

'I'm being very discreet, Syd.'

'I dunno, Cat.' He ran his hands through his hair distractedly. 'It's not right – you sittin' there all shaven and shorn.'

'I'm sorry, Syd,' I said, serious now, 'but it was the best we could come up with at such short notice. And after all, it's only hair: it'll grow back. I'm just staying here until the runners get tired of looking for me. If Hawkins goes away, they're bound to lose interest – there'll be no one to press charges.'

'Do you want me to get rid of 'im for you, Cat?' Syd's kind, open face became quite nasty for a moment. Used to him treating me like a wayward younger sister, I sometimes forgot that he ruled a fair percentage of London and could call on a powerful following.

'No, Syd. He won't be here forever. He's got his plantation in Jamaica to think of. Once he realizes he's not going to get hold of Pedro, he'll leave.'

'And what's the word? Does he show any signs of giving up?' Frank asked Syd.

'Nothin' doin' on that front as far as I've 'eard. I 'spect 'e's laying low since last night.' Syd's face broke into a grin. He took my hand affectionately and pulled me on to the arm of the chair beside him. 'Wasn't Prince a dazzler? 'Ole town is talkin' of it. Tonight's show is sold out. They could've flogged the tickets twice over, Caleb told me.' Syd's brow puckered again. ''E's worried for you too, Cat. Been lookin' for you when 'e's off duty. So's Pedro.'

'Can you let them know I'm all right?'

'Course I will.'

The bells in the abbey struck the hour. Syd got up to leave. He shook the boys by the hand. I held out mine. He took it but didn't shake it. Instead, he inspected the scratches I had sustained last night. "You're a rum 'un, Kitten. No two ways about it. You'll need to toughen up these paws of yours. And if you get in a fight, you're to aim 'ere and 'ere.' He pointed to Frank's jaw and stomach. 'You're not supposed to go lower, but if it's an emergency, punch or kick there . . .' (he pointed – Frank went pale) ' . . .as 'ard as you can. That should soon sort out your opponent. Goodnight.'

'Goodnight, Syd.'

The door closed.

'Anyone fancy something to eat?' asked Charlie, holding up a pan full of sizzling sausages.

SCENE 3 – SNATCHED

The following day was a Sunday and the boys from Westminster School were expected to attend the morning service in the Abbey. I ate cold sausages up in Frank's set rather than go down for breakfast. I'd decided that the less I was seen in public, the quicker people would forget about me. Charlie assured me that I wouldn't be missing much in the dining room.

Left alone for the first time, I sat in front of Frank's mirror and inspected my new appearance. My hair now curled around my ears. My neck felt strangely exposed. And my ankles. Despite being hidden in thick stockings, it felt so odd to have them on view. Indecent somehow. I experimented with some expressions. Boredom was the one I'd had most opportunity to study. Smiling was definitely out. As soon as I smiled, I became very girlie. A grimace was better.

'Very pretty, Hengrave.'

I spun round to find Richmond lounging in the doorway.

'Don't you know how to knock?' I asked, wondering with a panicky feeling how long he'd been standing there.

'Just came to see how the new boy was doing,' he said, inspecting a set of silver clothes brushes lying on a table.

'I'm doing fine, thank you.'

'You weren't at breakfast.'

'No.'

'Not sickening for something, I hope?'

'No.'

'Good. Then how would you like to join me for a spot of fencing in the Dean's Yard after church?'

'I don't fence.'

'Not a strict Sabbath observer, are you?' he asked with a curl to his lip.

'No.' I couldn't help smiling, thinking of what we got up to on Sundays at the theatre. That was the day I had the run of the place and got to play on stage, pretending I was Mrs Siddons or Mrs Jordan. Richmond gave me a strange look. I quickly turned off my smile. 'I mean I've never learned to fence.'

'Lord, Hengrave, are you savages in Ireland? Someone had better teach you then. By the old oak at midday.' And he turned on his heel and left before I could think of an excuse.

'Well, I suppose it was friendly of him,' said Frank, scratching the back of his head in bewilderment when I told him about my visitor. We were making the short journey across the yard to the Abbey, near deafened by the peal of bells.

'Friendly? Frank, I don't think so. I haven't been a boy long but I know when someone just wants to knock the stuffing out of me.'

Charlie shook his head. 'And it was the headmaster who accused us of having a talent for mischief, Frank. My little brother can't seem to stir without attracting trouble.'

'I think it's because of Tom Cat's looks,' said Frank sagely. 'Richmond's a bit of a runt himself, son of some planter from the West Indies. He's been struggling to find his feet in Ottley's from what Southey's told me. The assistant master there, Botch Hayes, can't keep the thugs under control and Richmond's been picked on. He's probably rejoicing in the fact that a boy has turned up who he stands a chance of thrashing. He sees you as a way to earn himself a bit of respect.'

'So you're saying I'm even runtier than Richmond, aren't you? Thanks, Frank. Remind me not to come to you for a compliment on another occasion.'

'And you've never fenced before?' asked Charlie.

I didn't think the question even deserved an answer. I merely raised my eyebrow.

'Of course not. Sorry.'

'But I have watched rehearsals for stage fights.' I neglected to mention that Pedro and I had also practised the moves afterwards when everyone had gone home.

'Well, it's the same principle, I expect,' said Frank. 'You need to learn the moves like in a dance.'

'I can dance,' I volunteered.

'Then you can fence. Don't worry. It'll just be practice swords – blunt ones. You might even like it.'

We entered the church. Being a cloudy winter's day outside, it was very dark in the Abbey. Little candles flickered in the side chapels like fireflies at dusk. The choir seemed a blaze of light in comparison to the rest of the pews as we shuffled forward to take our places. The choristers filed in, their scrubbed, shiny round faces floating on white ruffs. Then they began to sing and I forgot the dreary day. The singing was exquisite – so pure and penetrating. The anthem lifted me up to the carved roof and let me dance there like a butterfly in a shaft of sunlight.

'Cat, Cat.' The spell was broken by Frank

digging me in the ribs. 'Look, there's Pedro.'

I turned in my seat. Standing in the side aisle, listening with critical attention to the music, was my friend. He noticed me watching him. His eyes widened for a moment, he gave a small nod, and then moved towards a side chapel. I half got up but Charlie yanked me back.

'Stay where you are,' he whispered. 'The doctor will flay you if you leave the service.'

I looked to my left and saw the headmaster glaring in my direction. I bowed my head in a fit of fervent prayer.

'And look.' Frank nudged me again. A shifty-looking man with a red scarf had followed Pedro into the chapel. I recognized him well enough. All the runners and those in their pay were marked men in Covent Garden. Red Scarf was a familiar face, more usually to be seen worshipping at the bar of the Shakespeare Tavern than in a church such as this.

'It's one of the traps,' I whispered. 'A magistrate's man. He's tailing Pedro.'

'Of course he is. Wait till the end of the service. I'll think of something.'

From then on, no one could fault my piety. I sat with head bowed, nose in my prayer book, until the final anthem signalled the conclusion of the service.

'Right, I've an idea,' said Frank in a low voice. 'You hang back, Cat. Charlie, are you ready for the Captain Bennington-Smythe manoeuvre?'

Charlie grinned and nodded.

'What's the . . .?' But Frank was off, marching towards the magistrate's man as he lurked in the doorway to the antechapel.

'Captain Bennington-Smythe! What a surprise! I thought you were in Delhi with the Hussars!' Frank cried out, arms wide open to embrace his long-lost friend. 'Charlie, can you believe my luck? Not seen cousin Smythie for years and here he is!'

Red Scarf looked over his shoulder as the two boys bore down on him, clearly expecting to see a cavalry officer behind him. But there was no one. Frank seized the man's hand and pumped it up and down furiously.

'How are you, old man? Out of the Hussars now, eh? Sold your commission for a pretty penny, I've no doubt. Father always said it was a valuable position.'

The plain-clothes runner didn't know what to do. His cover was blown now that half of Westminster School was staring at him.

'I'm sorry, sir,' he said, tugging on his collar. 'You've got me mixed up with someone else.'

'Good one, Smythie!' Frank roared with laughter, slapping him on the back. 'He always did like his little joke,' he added to Charlie. 'You think I don't recognize my own third cousin twice removed when I see him, eh? Come, come, you must tell me all about it. I don't mind letting you know that I'm considering the army – Charlie too.'

'Absolutely,' beamed Charlie. 'So was it really hot in India? I've heard tales of eggs frying on the cannon. Is that true?'

'No – I mean I don't know,' blustered the man, who'd probably never been beyond Gravesend. 'Look, you've made a mistake . . .'

'You must tell us over a drink, old man,' said Frank, remorselessly towing his 'cousin' away. 'I dare say you've not lost your taste for a glass or two. You were always known as a capital topper.'

And 'Cousin' Smythie was propelled out of the Abbey doors, still protesting his ignorance of any kinship with Frank, as I slipped into the chapel. I touched Pedro on the arm.

'What was all that?' he asked, nodding to the door.

'A diversion – the magistrate's man was tailing you. Come on, let's get out of here.'

I pulled him to his feet and we ducked into Poets' Corner. There was a large marble tomb with weeping cherubs next to a statue of Shakespeare. I pulled Pedro with me into the space between it and the wall, comforted that we had our guardian bard keeping watch above.

'You look different,' said Pedro, giving my hand a squeeze.

'And you don't. How was the performance last night?'

'Good. But I didn't come here to talk about that. Oh Cat, what are we going to do about you?'

'Nothing for the moment. I'm safe where I am.'

'Safe? Hardly. You'll be found out.'

'I know, but it'll do for now. I'm hoping Hawkins will decide he's beaten and leave.'

Pedro shook his head. 'You don't know my master then. He never forgets – never forgives. I'm sorry I got you mixed up in all this.'

'Sorry? What have you got to be sorry about? It was me who rampaged through Brook's. I was so stupid.'

'But you were angry and frightened – you couldn't help it.'

'That won't count for anything with a judge, I'm afraid.'

'I suppose not.'

'You're being careful, aren't you?'

'Me? Of course. Syd's boys are escorting me to and from the theatre. I'm staying in Drury Lane or at Signor Angelini's, and never sticking my nose out of doors. I've got Joe and Nick waiting for me now outside.'

'Good.' Footsteps approached. We fell silent and waited for them to pass.

'You know,' I said once the coast was clear, 'I was thinking that if the worst comes to the worst I'll try to get to Johnny in America. He offered me a home, you know.'

'I remember. He probably realized it wouldn't be long before you did something really outrageous. He saw it brewing inside you.'

I dug him in the ribs for that. Pedro smiled.

'Yes, my sisters would have loved you,' he added. 'I know it's got you into very hot water, but at least you told Hawkins what you really thought of him. I wish I'd done that when I was his slave.'

'No, you don't. You wouldn't have lived if you

had. And you did do it on Friday in any case. You beat him good and proper in public.'

Pedro peered around the edge of the tomb. 'I'd better go. There's no knowing how long Frank's diversion will last.' He gave my hand a final squeeze. 'See you, Cat.'

'Goodbye, Pedro.'

I waited for him to disappear back into the Sunday crowds before crawling out from my hiding place. No sooner had I dusted myself down than a heavy hand landed on my shoulder, making me jump out of my skin.

'Hengrave! What are you doing, boy?' It was Mr Castleton, the Latin teacher.

'Just paying my respects to Shakespeare, sir,' I improvised. 'I've never been to Poets' Corner before.'

He let go of my shoulder. 'Hmm. You probably didn't know that you are now supposed to be in Bible study until noon. As it's your first week, I won't report you.' He tipped his hat to the bard and steered me back towards the main doors. 'You like Shakespeare, do you, Hengrave?'

'Yes, sir, I love him,' I replied honestly.

'I went to a most remarkable performance of *The Tempest* myself on Friday. "The cloud-capped towers, the gorgeous palaces . . . shall dissolve . . . Leave not a rack behind."'

'"We are such stuff

As dreams are made on; and our little life

Is rounded with a sleep,"' I finished for him.

Mr Castleton looked at me with approval. 'Poetry, my boy, poetry. I'm delighted to see you have learnt it by rote. It's the only way to get the rhythms into your heart. I suppose you went to the theatre in Dublin?'

'Occasionally,' I said with a smile. I had not had to learn that speech by rote; it was in my blood.

'Well, lad, if you're lucky, I might just take you to the home of drama itself – Theatre Royal, Drury Lane. There you'll see the very best actors of our age – Mr Kemble and his incomparable sister, Mrs Siddons. Would you like that?'

A lump had risen in my throat. 'I don't know, sir,' I said huskily.

'Well, I do. A boy like you who understands true poetry will be swept away by the experience. I would be proud to be the first to introduce you to the delights of the London stage.'

'Thank you, sir.' His kindness was alarming. He sounded as if he intended to carry out his promise. 'Perhaps next term?'

'Yes, yes, boy. Find your feet here first, eh? Is that what you're thinking?'

I nodded.

'I must remember you when it comes to casting the Latin play next week. You'd make a lovely Electra.'

'My Latin isn't all that good, sir. I don't think I'm up to appearing in a play,' I said hastily, not adding that I certainly didn't want to be cast as a girl.

'Nonsense! I can coach you in your part. You have the soul of the language – that's what counts. That's what makes the Westminster Latin play fit for kings! Indeed, the Prince of Wales himself is a great supporter – loves to see the Latin greats on the stage here at the school.'

As we descended the steps, I saw that Frank and Charlie had the unfortunate runner backed up against the porch.

'Come on, Smythie, you can't tell me you don't remember Ponsonby Wilmington. Good lord, man, he went to Delhi with you on the same ship,' Frank was saying.

'Look, sir, this has gone far enough.' The trap's face was now the same colour as his scarf. 'I'm not Captain What-yer-ma-call-it. I don't know any Ponsonby Wilmington. I've never been to India. I'm an officer of the law and you are obstructing my enquiries!'

Frank saw me emerging with Mr Castleton. He gave me a grin as he waited for me to pass.

'Do you know, Charlie, I think I may have made a mistake. Come to think of it, Captain Bennington-Smythe doesn't look anything like our man here, not since he had that wooden leg fitted. I'm awfully sorry to have inconvenienced you, officer. My mistake entirely.'

Frank and Charlie both shook the man solemnly by the hand.

'Carry on, officer, carry on,' said Charlie. 'So sorry to have detained you.'

And ignoring me and Mr Castleton, they turned tail and bolted into Westminster School before the runner had time to protest.

'Those two,' said the teacher with a shake of his head. 'Always up to something. What was that all about, I wonder?'

'I've no idea, sir,' I lied.

The midday bell released us from Bible study. I had hoped that Richmond had forgotten his desire to teach me fencing, but he looked over as we rose to leave the room and gave me a business-like nod.

'Don't worry, Cat. We'll come and make sure he plays fair,' said Frank, following my gaze.

'Avon, Hengrave Senior, come here!' Dr

Vincent had appeared in the door with a thunderous expression on his face. 'What's all this I hear about you accosting an officer of the law this morning?'

Charlie gave me a shove in the back. 'You'd better go in case our friend is somewhere about. We'll be along as soon as we can.'

Feeling very exposed without Charlie and Frank beside me, I crossed the quad to the archway leading to the Dean's Yard. Boys were pouring out of school in all directions, heading for the fields. Some had skates around their neck – the duck pond had frozen over in the night, promising capital sport. I would have much preferred to join them than take lessons from Richmond.

The old oak was not hard to spot. It leaned across the grass as if it hardly had the energy to stand upright. Two boys waited beneath its bare branches.

'It's just like *Twelfth Night*,' I muttered to myself. 'Viola dressed as a boy going to fight Sir Andrew Aguecheek.' The thought made me smile. My life had become like some absurd play – but at least that was something I could understand.

'Where's your big brother and your substance?' asked Richmond, looking over my shoulder to the archway. 'I thought you were too scared to be seen without them.'

'They're busy,' I said tersely.

'So, Hengrave, fancy yourself as a blade, do you?' Richmond threw me a thin practice sword.

'Not really.' I took a few swipes at the air to get the feel of it. It wasn't too heavy.

'I'll just teach you the rudiments today.' Richmond's eyes were glinting with an evil light. 'Nothing too taxing for a sickly specimen like you.'

'I'm not sickly.'

'No? We'll see. Hold your blade up in the guard position. Yes, that's it. You'll find it easier with your jacket off.'

'I'm all right as I am, thank you.'

Richmond took off his own jacket and threw it to Ingels. 'I suppose you're too prim to be seen in your shirtsleeves. You are a queer fellow, Hengrave.'

I said nothing. I had clearly made another error in my boyish behaviour. Unbuttoning my jacket, I hung it over a lower branch of the tree and turned to face my adversary.

'Now, watch me – here's the first move.' Stepping forward quickly, Richmond brought his blade up to mine with a tap, tap. 'Try to gain ground so that you keep the initiative, see?' He lunged towards me. I backed away. 'Now, you try.'

My memory of the moves used in stage fights came greatly to my assistance as Richmond drilled me in the basics of fencing. He did not depart from his script as teacher. I almost began to think that he had meant nothing malicious by his invitation to introduce me to the sport. I was wrong.

'Right, I think you know enough now to try a practice fight.' Richmond paused, wiping his forehead on the back of his sleeve and glancing around the yard to check we were unobserved.

'What?' I let my sword trail on the ground.

Richmond darted forward and prodded me hard in the ribs. I yelped. 'Never drop your guard, Hengrave. Come on, a quick fight just to drive home what you've learned.'

'I'm not sure . . .'

'He's scared,' grunted Ingels.

'I'm not!' I retorted.

'Then prove it,' challenged Richmond.

Ladies, you should know that being a boy is very complicated. To maintain my honour I would have to fight, but that would result in a very humiliating defeat, I had no doubt. I held my sword in the guard position.

'That's better. En garde!'

Richmond let himself go at me with a hail of blows. I parried the first two, but then took several to my body. The last one smashed down on my fingers, bringing tears to my eyes. I dropped the sword and cradled my hand, anger buzzing inside me.

'As I said yesterday, new boys should re-member their place,' said Richmond, breaking off his attack and giving me a mirthless smile. 'I expect you to show me more respect next time, Hengrave.'

'Respect? Don't make me laugh! You're nothing but a pisspot bully, Richmond,' I spat. He went white but I'm afraid my temper had run away with me now and I couldn't stop my mouth. 'Think you're so clever, don't you? Well, all I can say is you're overdue a thrashing, you . . . you gadso!'

And I grabbed my jacket from the branch and strode off as fast as I could back to my rooms.

I was still fuming as I crashed into the room and threw myself into a chair. My side was covered in bruises and my hand still smarted from the blow. I hated being a boy. I so wanted to be back home at Drury Lane with my own people, not masquerading among bullying rich boys and cane-obsessed teachers. I covered my face with my hands and gave vent to the furious tears that had been waiting to spill.

Footsteps came up the stairs and the door opened. I wiped my face on my sleeve but it was too late.

'Cat? What happened?' Frank came in and crouched before me. Then he saw the slash across my knuckles and swore.

'I'll kill him,' muttered Charlie, grinding his fist into his palm.

'Richmond's a wart on the face of humanity,' I said angrily, blowing my nose. 'I don't know what they put in the water in the West Indies but he's clearly from the same school as Pedro's old master. But don't you do anything. This is between him and me.' Frank got to his feet and winced. 'What's wrong with you?' I asked.

'Nothing the Avon rear protector could not have handled, but unfortunately we did not go to church prepared,' said Frank regretfully.

'I'm sorry. This is all my fault,' I groaned.

'Absolutely, Cat, but it's worth every minute of pain. I've never known school to be so exciting.'

Frank smiled, challenging me to cheer up.

I grimaced. 'I think it's war between me and Richmond. I called him a gadso. I've never called anybody a gadso before but it just slipped out.'

'Oh dear,' said Frank, struggling to hide a grin.

'What's a gadso?' asked Charlie.

'One of the riper words of Covent Garden indicating a rather delicate part of the male anatomy, suggesting that the subject has nothing else in his skull,' explained Frank.

'Oh.' Charlie grinned. 'I'll remember that. Cat, thanks for broadening my education.'

I gave a grim smile. 'Stick around me, Charlie, and it'll be so broad you won't be able to see the edges.'

If Richmond was meditating his revenge, he was taking his time about it. I begged Frank to continue my fencing training in case of further challenges but nothing happened to call on my new skills. The following weeks passed without incident, not even a near escape. The other boys had accepted me as part of Frank and Charlie's circle of friends and ceased to pay particular attention to me. I even avoided having to act for the older boys as a skivvy – or 'fag' in schoolboy parlance – for Frank had made it clear that I was his and Charlie's personal dogsbody. Not that Frank would have got away with giving me orders had the mood taken him. Wisely, he didn't dare.

Settling into my role, I was amused to find out more about Frank's life at school. Being the son of a duke placed him at the top of the social ladder, so he did not have to try hard to earn respect like the rest of us. He had, however, gained himself a notoriety all of his own which was nothing to do with his blue blood. Known as 'The Wizard' to the other boys, I was amazed to find that Frank had introduced into Westminster some of the skills he had picked up from his acquaintances in Covent Garden. He augmented his income by forging letters from parents for needy pupils, and had been known to rewrite reports home from the teachers. His mastery of Dr Vincent's hand was particularly commended. He had a little business going with Nick, Syd's second-in-command and apprentice to a shoemaker, who supplied him with the supple leather required for the manufacture of the Avon Rear Protector. Nick's sister, a seamstress, sewed the false lining in the seat of the breeches belonging to the young gentlemen, taking the sting out of the flogging administered by that lover of the rod, Dr Vincent. Frank's rooms were a hive of activity with pupils coming and going with requests for Frank's aid in the various trials of their life at school. All I had to do was sit in the shadows and watch.

By the end of the second week, my academic career was developing in leaps and bounds. Mr Castleton had ranked me tenth in the form for my knowledge of Latin. Not the grammar, he explained to his listeners, of which I showed a very shaky grasp, but the true poetry of it.

'This boy is the only one who really understands. Watch him and learn!' he declared as he got me to read out a verse aloud. That was easy. My training at Drury Lane made this child's play. 'See, he's reading it as if he means it – not murdering it as the rest of you do. Now, Southey, you translate.'

But this proved to be a temporary lull. Life got much more complicated as November turned into December. It was a glorious winter's day with cold, blue skies, and we had been given some free time as lessons finished early. Frank and Charlie decided to go snipe hunting in Tothill Fields. I'd begged off, saying I wanted to spend more time with my Latin books.

'No need to work so hard, Cat. You're doing fine from what I hear,' said Frank. 'Rookie's very impressed by you. Why not take a holiday and come and watch?'

'No thanks. I really want to read.'

'Proof, if ever you need it,' he said, shaking his head in disbelief, 'that you're not the real thing, Cat. No self-respecting boy would sit in on a day like this.'

'Get lost, my lord,' I said, throwing a cushion at him.

Frank didn't understand what a luxury it was to have time to study uninterrupted. At the theatre I had had to squeeze my education into my spare time. It had been somewhat neglected since Mr Salter, no friend of mine, had replaced Johnnie as prompt. His idea of educating me was to set me the grate in his office to shine with blacklead while he delivered lectures on female virtue from Fordyce's sermons. He had made it clear to Mr Sheridan and Mr Kemble that he thought it very dangerous to teach a girl of my class because it would raise me above my allotted station in life. However, they had insisted he continue the work begun by his predecessors. They probably thought they were doing me a favour, but if I hear another word written by the insufferable Fordyce, I'll scream.

So I liked the change I had unexpectedly

made to a life devoted to study. Hidden in Westminster School with my books, I could pass the time with the gods, fight on the battlefields of Troy, or wander the world with Aeneas. This was all the holiday I needed.

Much sooner than I had expected, I heard footsteps returning back up the stairs. Someone coughed loudly outside the door.

'Wait a moment, I'll just check that our room mate is prepared to receive visitors,' said Charlie loudly.

'Oh Milly, you must see the view from the window over here.' I heard Lizzie say.

'I can't see anything special. It looks out on a brick wall.' This last voice belonged to a stranger.

Charlie slipped through the door. 'My sister's here, Cat. Lizzie brought her in the carriage when she called in to leave a parcel for Frank with the porter. I've been trying to keep her happy with a tour of the whole damn school, but she insists on seeing my rooms. Just follow my lead, all right?'

'But she'll know I'm not your brother, Charlie!' I looked about me, wondering if it were feasible to take to my bed with a sudden fever.

'Of course she will. No, for her, you're just another boy.'

'Really, Lizzie, I can't see anything remarkable about those bricks,' said Milly. The door was opening. I messed up my hair and assumed my best bored expression. 'So these are your rooms, Charlie. Very nice. So much light up here.' A girl of Lizzie's age glided into the room. She was dressed in a deep red cape with fur round the hood. Her dark eyes darted from side to side with lively attention to every detail. Lizzie followed, wearing her pretty grey spenser jacket and muff. Our eyes met. An expression of consternation passed across her face. Did I really look that shocking? She turned her gaze away.

'Ladies,' said Charlie formally, bowing to them. 'May I introduce our room mate Tom . . . Cat Smith.'

I bowed clumsily.

'Tom Cat? What a peculiar name?' commented Milly, staring at me through her long black lashes.

'It's a nickname,' Frank jumped in quickly. 'His full name is Thomas Bennington-Smythe. I'm looking after him this term: he's my shadow.'

Milly gave me a smile. 'What a sweet little boy. He does look a bit like a kitten, doesn't he, Lizzie, with those big green eyes?'

'Er, yes,' said Lizzie quickly, her gaze gliding over me as if she did not know where to look. I flushed with embarrassment.

'How old are you, child? You look very young to be at this school.'

'He's only two years below me, Milly, though he is one of the smallest,' said Charlie.

'Do you like school, Tom Cat?' She was talking to me as if I was barely out of the nursery.

'Yes, thank you, miss,' I replied gruffly.

'You know, I've got a brother your age. He's called Thomas too.'

'Shouldn't we be going?' interrupted Lizzie,

pulling on her friend's arm. 'The Miss Millers will be waiting for us.'

'They won't mind if we're a bit late,' Milly replied, taking the chair I had just vacated. 'Now, how about rustling your sister up a cup of tea, Charlie?'

There seemed no shifting her. Charlie pretended he had run out of tea but Milly sniffed out the caddy in a trice and put the kettle on the fire herself.

'Anyone would think you weren't pleased to have visitors, Charlie,' Milly said with a laugh. 'Don't you want to hear how the Movement is getting on? You were all fired up with enthusiasm for it last week when there was the African boy to champion.'

'I still am,' said Charlie, urging the kettle on to steam so that tea could be dispensed as quickly as possible.

'And what about you, Mr Tom Cat?' Milly had clearly taken a fancy to my nickname. 'Are you a supporter of the cause?'

'Yes, indeed, miss,' I said, wishing she wouldn't keep smiling at me as I was trying to keep to my boyish sulks.

'Then perhaps you'd like one of these?' She took from her capacious reticule a flat pottery disc about the size of my palm. 'It's made by Mr Wedgwood's manufactory.' I took it from her and saw that it was decorated on one side with a kneeling African in chains. Surrounding him were the words 'Am I not a man and a brother?' – a line from one of my favourite anti-slavery poems by Cowper.

'Thank you, miss.'

'Well, they're a guinea each. We're selling them to raise money for our work.' She gave me an expectant look.

'Oh.' I blushed an even deeper shade of red. I didn't have a guinea – just the loose change that Mr Sheridan had thrust into my hand up in the Sparrow's Nest and there was no gold among those coins.

'Here, I've got some money. You can pay me

back later, Tom Cat,' said Frank quickly.

'Thanks.' The medallion now seemed to be burning my hand as I stuffed it into my jacket. Unfortunately, Milly did not have a tactful bone in her body. Her attempts to make amends for putting me on the spot only made things worse.

'I do apologize, Mr Tom Cat. Of course, I should have thought that you might not have the means to pay out such a sum. I should have asked Charlie first.'

'It's all right, miss.'

'No, it's not. I can see I mortified you. You must never be embarrassed by lack of means.' She cocked her head to one side, examining me closely. 'I've no doubt your father is an honourable man much respected in the circles he moves in, despite financial constraints. Am I right?'

'I am an orphan, miss,' I said sullenly.

'Oh lord, worse and worse! Please forgive me. My family are always telling me that when I get myself in a hole, I must stop digging, but I don't seem able to somehow. I have an instinct for saying the wrong thing, you could say. So, Mr Tom Cat, you must have a very kind patron who pays your fees, I suppose? Some decent man of good family? You must count yourself very fortunate.'

Her curiosity was relentless. She seemed determined to winkle out of me my family connections. It may have been merely the concern of a sister trying to check that her brother was mixing with the right sort; it may have been that she was plain nosy. I could hardly blame her because curiosity was a sin of which I certainly was guilty.

'Indeed, miss, I have two very kind patrons without whom I wouldn't be here today.' I gave Frank and Charlie a sly grin.

'That's better. I'm so pleased to see you smile. I thought I had quite sent you into the doldrums with my foolishness.'

We all watched her drink her tea with hawkish interest. As soon as she had drained her cup, Charlie leapt to his feet.

'Now that you've finished, let me show you to your carriage, Milly.'

'My word, Charlie, you're in a hurry to get rid of us, aren't you?'

'Not at all, sis, not at all. It's just that . . .' Charlie fished around for a plausible excuse.

'We've got fencing practice in a few minutes and we need to change,' said Frank quickly.

'Well, in that case, we'd better go. You watch my brother, Mr Tom Cat,' Milly said playfully as she rose. 'He never showed me any mercy when we were children in the nursery together so I hate to think what he'd do to a boy like you.'

'Sis, you know that's not true. If I remember, you were the one who was lethal with the hatpin at a very young age,' protested Charlie.

'Self-defence, Charles, self-defence . . .'

The voices of the Hengraves faded as Charlie led his sister back to the lodge, leaving me alone with the Avons for a few moments.

'How are you, Cat?' Lizzie said, her voice trembling slightly. 'I mean, really?'

I gave her a brave smile but her kindness made me feel weak. 'I'm homesick,' I confessed.

'Are they treating you well? No one suspects anything?'

'She's doing brilliantly, Lizzie,' said Frank. 'Completely convincing.'

'But what are you going to do?'

'Do? I'm aiming to be top in my form for Latin and to become a passable fencer,' I joked feebly.

'Cat, you know what I mean. You can't stay here forever.'

Milly called Lizzie's name from the bottom of the stairs. She straightened her bonnet in the mirror, and tidied her curls ready to leave. I touched my shorn head self-consciously. It was then that the idea hit me.

'Lizzie, could you help me with something?'

'Of course. Anything.'

'Can you send me some things? I might need them at short notice.' I moved to Frank's desk and began a list. 'I'll write them down for you.'

Lizzie read the list quickly and gave a nod.

'I'll send them round tomorrow. Is that all you need?'

'Yes. And thank you.'

She hesitated, then gave me a swift kiss. 'It feels so strange kissing a boy!' she said with a small laugh and let Frank escort her back to the carriage.

Milly's visit turned out to be but the prelude to something far worse. Frank and Charlie took a long time coming back from the lodge and I began to worry what had happened to them. Perhaps they had met another pupil, or worse a teacher, and Milly had been asked about how she found her younger brother? Would there be footsteps thundering up the stairs any moment now, demanding to know who the impostor was? I listened by the door, tensing myself to make a run for it if necessary. Sure enough, I heard pounding footsteps. I hid behind the door, ready to flee as soon my chance came.

'Cat! Cat!' It wasn't a teacher or the porter as I had half expected: it was just Frank and Charlie, both of them white as a sheet.

'Is someone after me?' I asked hastily, craning my head out on to the landing, listening for more footsteps.

'No.' Frank hauled me back in by the jacket and closed the door with a bang. 'Look. The boy was just crying the news as we handed Lizzie and Milly into the carriage.' He thrust a newspaper into my hand. The front page was covered in advertisements, but my eyes lit upon the headline.

Mysterious disappearance of the African Ariel

Tonight's performance of *The Tempest* at Drury Lane has had to be cancelled due to the mysterious disappearance of the African known as *Pedro Hawkins*. He went missing some time after four o'clock Tuesday afternoon from the house of his current master, *Signor Luigi Angelini*. No one saw the

African leave the house. Pedro Hawkins' fate has been an issue of great public concern since it has become known that *a former master* claims to own the young African. Immediate enquiries were made with the gentleman in question, but he denied all knowledge of the boy's whereabouts and permitted officers of the law to search his lodgings to prove his innocence.

In place of the advertised programme, Drury Lane will be performing *Macbeth*.

I sat down heavily in the armchair. 'We didn't save him after all.'

Frank slammed his hand down on the mantelpiece in frustration. 'I thought he was safe! He was being guarded on the streets and staying indoors, but he's been snatched anyway!'

Charlie squeezed my shoulder. 'Lizzie and Milly have gone straight to Mr Sharp's. The abolitionists will do all they can.'

'What *can* they do?' I asked.

'Mr Sharp can apply in the courts for *habeas corpus* – it's a court order that means that Hawkins will have to produce Pedro if he has him. Mr Sharp's used it before to stop men being taken out of England against their will.'

'But Hawkins claims he doesn't have him. What good will this habeas thing do if he can get away with pretending he knows nothing about it?'

Charlie fell silent. They both knew I was right. It had to be Hawkins – of course it did – but clearly he had hidden Pedro somewhere with the intent of bypassing the legal channels to get him out of the country. After his humiliation at Drury Lane, Hawkins had probably decided the public pressure to keep Pedro here was too strong for him to fight overtly. He was trying to smuggle Pedro away.

'We need to act fast,' I said, my mind clicking into action. 'We've got to get our friends to check the port. It's the obvious place. If he's not sent Pedro there yet, he will.' I closed my eyes, leaning back in the chair, fighting my panic and fear. I was useless. I couldn't even go to Covent Garden to get a message to Syd and the gang. In Pedro's hour of need, I was stuck learning Latin and pretending to be an Irish landowner's younger son.

'I'll go,' said Frank, getting up. 'Make my excuses at Prep for me, Charlie. I've suddenly developed a bad toothache and gone home to see the family tooth puller.'

'Right you are,' said Charlie.

'And, Cat, stay put! Charlie, make sure she does!' Frank said, realizing exactly what I was thinking as I sat there with my eyes tight shut. 'You won't help Pedro by getting caught yourself, Cat. The gang'll look after him – you'll see.'

I nodded, but something told me that it would need more than the Butcher's Boys to find him. As Pedro had warned, Hawkins never forgot and never forgave – he was not a man to let revenge on his slave be denied him.

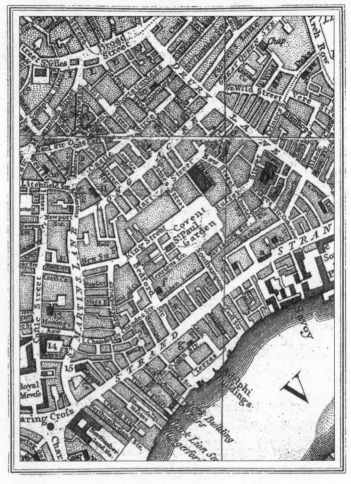

*Act III - In which Billy
Shepherd takes our heroine for a walk
in the moonlight ...*

ACT III

SCENE 1 – WOLFSBANE FOR BRUISES

Frank did not come back that night. I suspected that he had returned to the streets of London to help search for Pedro. I wished I could join him. Charlie was straining at the leash too; only his sense of duty to me stopped him from going. By common consent, neither of us talked about it as we sat by the fire. My mind was too vividly imagining what might be happening to Pedro. I felt sick with anxiety.

'Well, little brother, I think you'd better turn in for the night,' Charlie said with an attempt at light-heartedness. 'I'll wake you if Frank returns with any news.'

Glumly, I did as I was told. It made no sense to sit up staring at the coals. I eventually fell asleep sometime after the Abbey bells tolled midnight. Immediately, Pedro appeared in my dreams – or should I say my nightmares. He was flying up to the sky on his harness, wings fluttering behind him, waving to me. I waved back. Then a sword appeared out of nowhere and sliced through the rope that held him. Pedro plummeted to the floor, screaming.

'Are you all right?' Charlie was standing beside me in his nightshirt, holding a candle.

'Y-yes. What's the matter?' I couldn't remember where I was for a moment, thinking myself back in the Sparrow's Nest. Memory returned. 'Is Frank here yet?'

'No. It's just that you screamed.'

I slumped back on my pillow. 'Sorry. I was having a nightmare – about Pedro.'

Charlie nodded. 'I'm not surprised. I couldn't sleep for thinking of him. I'll get you a glass of water. Try and get some rest.'

He came back with the glass and placed it on the bedside table.

'Drink this. You can't do any more than you've already done for Pedro.' He sat on the bed beside me. 'Try not to fret, little brother. I'll stay here until you're asleep. Don't worry: you're safe with us.'

The water helped – more because of Charlie's kindness thinking of it than because I was thirsty – but it couldn't dull the acute ache of homesickness for Drury Lane and my fear for Pedro. Where was he now?

The following day, Charlie went out early to see if the newspapers carried any more stories about Pedro. There was a short piece on the front page – an appeal by Mr Sharp and Mr Equiano for any information leading to the discovery of the African Ariel – but nothing else.

'I'm going to send a message to Milly,' Charlie told me over breakfast in the great dining room. 'I want to find out what the Movement's decided to do.'

As he left, I smoothed the page out and stared at the bald words before me – 'the African', 'former slave', 'missing' – Pedro had been reduced to a paragraph. It said nothing about my friend, his talents, his quick laugh. The real boy had disappeared too as far as the public were concerned, becoming just an interesting story about a runaway slave. I took out the pottery medallion and looked at the man depicted on its face. It struck me then that, despite Mr Wedgwood's best efforts, this African also seemed a caricature – a clumsy representative of thousands of suffering individuals whose stories would probably never be known.

'Morning, Hengrave.' Richmond plumped himself down on the bench beside me, slopping porridge on my newspaper. 'Oops! So sorry about that. What's that you're fondling?'

'None of your business,' I said sharply, hiding the medallion under the table.

'Something you're not supposed to have, I don't doubt. A picture of your girlfriend – or your boyfriend perhaps?' Fatty Ingels pushed his way on to the bench on the other side of me, squeezing me between them.

'Very funny, I don't think,' I said, trying to get up.

Four or five other boys came to sit around us, all grinning at me. I didn't know them, but I recognized Richmond's set – all sons of plantation owners who knew each other from the West Indies. It seemed that Richmond had succeeded in finding himself a place in the school pecking order: at the head of a group of fellow bullies who liked persecuting runty shadows from rival boarding houses, namely yours truly.

'I hear you and your brother are upset over the disappearance of a certain negro,' said Richmond loudly, spraying me with porridge from his mouth.

'What makes you think that?' I asked as calmly as I could muster.

'Oh, Ingels here heard the commotion in the lodge yesterday when the news broke. Had your sister in a fit of the vapours, he said, screaming and crying like a baby. Now I know where you get it from.'

'You leave my sister out of this,' I said, standing and making to leave. Richmond gave a nod to his friends and they rose as one to follow me. If life in Covent Garden has taught me one thing, it is to recognize a gang when I see it. I started to stride quickly, heading towards the Lower Form classroom where I hoped they dare not pursue me.

'You know, Hengrave, I really am interested in seeing what you were looking at,' said Richmond, catching me up and taking my arm. I shook him off and broke into a run. I could hear the thunder of feet behind me. I took a sharp left, then a right, trying to lose them, but they were on my scent like a pack of hounds. What should I do? At home, I would've known every alleyway, every house, and would've given them the slip easily; here I was on foreign territory. I ducked round the corner of a building and saw a door immediately ahead of me at the end of a narrow passage. I ran straight for it, but it was locked. I turned back. My enemies were massed in front of me, blocking my exit. I was trapped.

'Nowhere to go, eh, Hengrave?' said Richmond, sauntering up to me, his face alight with malice. Away from his plantation, he must have missed having someone to persecute and was making up for lost time. 'Now hand over whatever it was you were looking at.'

Blank windows looked down on the blind alley I had turned into. No friendly face from Clough's appeared above to come to my rescue. There seemed no point in resisting. It was only a piece of pottery after all. I unclenched my fist and held it out on my palm. Richmond bent down to take a closer look and let out a howl of laughter.

'"Am I not a man and a brother?" – well, not you, Hengrave, you nan boy.' He slapped my hand away and turned to his followers. 'Gentlemen, we have an abolitionist in our midst. And what do we think of that crew?'

'Dirty thieves!' grunted one.

'And do you know what this thief called me

on Sunday? A name so foul I'd blush to repeat it.'
Richmond raised his eyes heavenwards in mock
piety. 'What do we do to foul-mouthed little boys
in our school, just as we do to runaway slaves
at home?'

'Teach them a lesson. Make them eat dirt!'
said a freckle-faced boy twice my height.

'That's right.' 'Let him have what's coming to
him!' The chorus of voices swelled around me.

My heart was racing. I couldn't take them all
on. Even Syd's emergency manoeuvre would not
help me.

'Kneel, Hengrave,' commanded Richmond.

'W-what?' I stammered, fearing my legs
would give way at any moment in any case.

'Like the negro on this piece of rubbish.
Kneel to your masters.'

That stiffened my sinews if nothing else could.

'I'd rather kiss a monkey's bum than kneel
to you.'

'My, my, you do have a colourful turn of
phrase, don't you, Hengrave? I think we should

make an example of you, just as will be done to that negro boy when his rightful master gets him back home. It'll teach others of your persuasion that spreading the poison of the abolition will not go unpunished.'

'No, don't . . . please.' I held out my hands in front of me to ward him off. It cost me to beg anything from him but I had no choice.

'Then kneel.'

Deciding discretion was the better part of valour, I sank to my knees, hoping this would satisfy him. But he hadn't finished with me: he'd only just started. Fixing his eyes on mine, he grabbed a handful of mud and rubbed it into my mouth, gripping the back of my neck as I struggled against him. The other boys cheered.

'That's better,' he said, wiping his hands on my jacket. 'Now you know who's master here.' Trembling with fury, I spat at his feet. 'Not yet learned your lesson? Take this, you dog!' He aimed a kick, catching me in the stomach. I instinctively curled up into a ball, my hands protecting my head, as the others joined in, treating me like – well, like one of their slaves. Pain flashed through me again and again. I probably screamed but I can't remember much more – except that the kicks stopped as suddenly as they had started when a voice thundered overhead:

'Stop that this instant! Leave that boy alone!' My persecutors fled as the locked door was flung open from inside and I saw a pair of boots inches from my face. Mr Castleton bent down.

'Good God, is that you, Hengrave?' The thought fluttered in my mind that this was a stupid question really in the circumstances and it was one that I did not answer as I blacked out.

I awoke and found myself lying on an unfamiliar bed in a room with a high ceiling. The air was cold and fresh. Someone was taking my boots off.

'Back with us? That's good.' A woman in an apron and cap was smiling at me from the far end of the bed: it was Mrs Clough, dame of my house and the person I had been trying to avoid since my first day.

'What happened? What am I doing here?' I asked groggily.

'I'd say you were set upon by some bullies. I see it all the time. Little chaps like you always seem to bear the brunt of it. Mr Castleton found you and carried you in here. He told me you weigh no more than a feather. Looks as though you've not been eating well, young man.' She wagged a finger at me.

'I've been ill,' I said, remembering my family history.

'That explains it, poor lamb. Now tell me, do you think anything's broken? Your nose looks undamaged – that's usually the first thing to go on these occasions.'

In a fog of pain, I moved my arms and legs on her instructions. They hurt like fury but were in working order.

'You'll live, Hengrave,' she said with a nod that set the ribbons on her cap dancing. 'Now, let's see to those bruises. I've got some wolfsbane which will sort them out in no time. It'll draw out the bruises. Take off your shirt.'

I sat up in more of a hurry than was wise, almost blacking out again with the pain. 'No, I don't need it,' I said hastily.

'Come, come, boy, no need to be shy. I've seen hundreds of boys in the flesh.'

Not like me, she hadn't.

'No, really, if you'll just let me get back to my rooms, I'll be all right.'

'Don't be a fool, Hengrave. You're not going anywhere for the rest of the day. Now take off your shirt.'

A door banged open at the far end of the room and Charlie galloped into sight.

'Mrs Clough, how's my brother?' he asked, giving me a desperate look.

'Well, he's just had what you barbarian boys call a good kicking, but he'll live. He's now refusing to let me put some wolfsbane on his bruises. How he expects to get better if he won't take his medicine, I don't know. Tell him to take his shirt off like a good boy, will you?'

Charlie quickly grasped my predicament.

'He's very shy, Mrs Clough. It'll be torture for him to do that in front of you. What needs doing?'

'All I want to do is rub some ointment on his bruises.' She took another look at my shocked face. 'But I don't want to make him suffer any more today, so you do it for me, Hengrave.' She put a jar in his hand. 'I'll leave you in peace so that his delicate sensibilities are not offended by the presence of a female.' She tutted and left the room.

Silence fell. I could hear the bustle of the school beyond the peaceful sanatorium. Boys were calling to each other as they went to the first lesson. Charlie held the jar gingerly as if it might explode at any moment. Our situation suddenly struck me as being so absurd it was funny. Mrs Clough thought I had an aversion to females! I began to giggle hysterically but stopped as my ribs ached.

'Who was it, Cat?' Charlie asked. His voice was taut with suppressed anger.

'Richmond and his planter friends from Ottley's. Teaching me a lesson about abolition.' I winced. 'Are you going to pass me that ointment then?' He handed it to me wordlessly. 'Turn your back, please.' I took a scoop from the jar and began to rub my battered body. They had certainly been thorough. I couldn't reach my shoulder blades which had taken the brunt of the attack. 'Er, Charlie, would you mind helping your little brother rub this on his back?'

He blushed as red as I did. 'Of course. I'll keep my eyes closed.' He swiftly applied the wolfsbane. Neither of us spoke, but finally Charlie burst out, 'I'm going to beat Richmond into a pulp when I see him.'

'What good will that do?' I asked, feeling tired of this whole charade. More than anything I wanted to be back among my own people – back at Drury Lane.

'Well, it'll make me feel a lot better for a start.'

Mrs Clough bustled back in. 'Now get yourself into that bed, Hengrave. I want to keep you here until I'm happy you'll not black out again.'

'Cat . . . my brother was kicked unconscious?' asked Charlie, his knuckles white as he gripped the jar.

'Yes, dear, but he'll be all right now with me to look after him. Run along to lessons. You can come back later to check on him.' She handed me a nightshirt and left the room.

'Right, that's it. This is war,' Charlie declared in a hiss as he stood with his back to me, his shoulders quivering with rage. 'Those slavers won't know what's hit them.'

'Charlie, don't. They're not worth it,' I whispered hoarsely.

'But you are,' he said, leaving the room abruptly.

I put the nightshirt over my breeches and got into bed. The wolfsbane did indeed have a soothing effect on my bruises and I fell asleep, dreaming the morning away. I only woke up when someone touched my arm gently. Fearing it was Mrs Clough coming to apply the ointment again, I sat up quickly, gathering the sheets around me.

'Don't worry, Cat, it's only me,' said Frank, not quite meeting my eyes. He looked tired. 'And I've brought you a visitor.'

I turned to find the Duchess of Avon sitting at my bedside.

'Oh no.' I collapsed back on the pillow. So it had all come out then.

The duchess leaned forward and kissed me on the cheek. 'Don't be alarmed, Master Tom Cat, I've heard all about it from Frank and Lizzie. I assure you that I have no interest in interfering with your decision to – how shall we put it? – play a breeches role for a few weeks. I merely came to bring back Frank and leave the items you requested – and perhaps catch sight of you in your new guise. But when we arrived, we learned you had ended up here, so I changed my role as messenger into that of sick bed visitor. I hope that is not unwelcome?'

I shook my head and flinched with the pain. Frank, failing to disguise his outrage at finding me like this, took to striding up and down the room.

'Is there any news?' I asked.

'Of your little African friend? No, I'm sorry to say,' said the duchess softly.

'Nothing?' I turned to Frank.

'We've looked everywhere in Covent Garden,' said Frank. 'He's not there. Syd's spoken to the boys from Billingsgate and they're searching the port. So far, no news. All we know is that Pedro stayed at home all day and the only visitors to the house were a blind piano tuner and his assistant at four in the afternoon. Pedro met them and showed them into the music room. According to the maid, these two showed themselves out later when they'd finished. We're trying to find them because it sounds as if they were the last people to see Pedro. Joe 'The Card' thinks he knows where the blind man lives. Somewhere near Seven Dials, he says, so we have to tread carefully.'

Seven Dials – that was in an area known as the Rookeries, Billy Shepherd's patch, the haunt of thieves, beggars and vagrants. I was sceptical that even Joe would find the blind man if he thought it in his interests to vanish for a while. Then something Richmond had said before the kicking came back to me. 'One of the boys that attacked me seemed to know a lot about Pedro. He said that Pedro's old master was planning to get him home and make an example of him as a warning to other runaways.'

Frank stopped pacing. 'He said that, did he? How would he know?'

'He talked about it as if it were an open secret among the slavers. They all seem to be aware of what's planned, even if they don't know the details.'

The duchess stroked my arm. 'It's very possible. The planters have joined forces to oppose Mr Wilberforce.'

'I wouldn't be surprised if they were all in on it,' Frank said, running his fingers through his hair in exasperation. 'Pedro's become something of a test case for both sides.'

The duchess sighed heavily. 'If the slavers can get him out of England, the laws of slavery apply once more. He's no longer a servant but a slave again, God help him.' She leant forward and smoothed my hair off my brow. 'What are we going to do with you? Shall I see if I can get you transferred to our house so we can look after you? It would certainly save you a lot of trouble here.'

It was a very attractive offer – with only one drawback.

'Have the runners stopped looking for me?'

'I don't know, sweetheart. They've talked to the servants a couple of times, according to Joseph.'

'Do you think any of them would tell on me if they knew I was in the house?'

The duchess frowned. 'What do you think, Frankie?'

Frank chewed his bottom lip. 'It's a very large staff we have, Mama. I don't know all of them. It would be risky. Cat's probably safer here for the moment.'

'What a shame.' The duchess touched one of my curls tenderly. 'You know, it rather suits you cropped. Long hair can be such a bore. I always prefer a wig – so much more convenient – but that's a secret best kept between you, me and the hairdresser.' With that, she rose to her feet and kissed me on the brow. 'I was almost forgetting – here's your parcel from Lizzie. What would you like me to do with it?'

'Can you give it to Frank to take up to my room? It had better not stay here. If someone opened it, I'd have some very awkward questions to answer.'

His mother gone, Frank finally met my eyes.

'Dammit, Cat, can't you keep out of trouble for five minutes?' he said. Though he sounded angry, I knew he was just furious with himself for failing to protect me.

'You know me, Frank. If there's trouble anywhere on hand, I'll walk right into it. Us runty fellows seem to attract it like magnets – even Mrs Clough said so.'

'Runty! I never said you were runty. I may have implied you were a bit undersized, but that's not surprising –'

'What was it Milly said yesterday?' I interrupted. 'When you're in a hole, stop digging?'

Frank smiled, recognizing the justice of my remark.

'I'm sorry I wasn't there, Cat.'

'And I'm sorry I was. Try to stop Charlie doing anything stupid in retaliation, won't you? Richmond might be a valuable source of information on Pedro. I wouldn't want his mouth permanently shut in some misguided attempt to avenge me.'

Frank nodded and chucked me under the chin in parting. 'Chin up, Tom Cat. You're certainly playing the part properly. Now you've been beaten black and blue, no one can say you didn't experience the full delights of boyhood.'

SCENE 2 – BILLY SHEPHERD RETURNS

Charlie was waiting with me outside the head-master's office. I had been called in to explain how I had been rendered unconscious.

'What would a boy say?' I whispered to Charlie. 'Would he tell?'

'Lord no, Cat. Your life will be hell if you are thought to have snitched. You leave Richmond and his crew to us boys. You should say something like you "tripped" or you "fell down the stairs".'

'But Mr Castleton saw them.'

'Yes, but the teachers don't expect you to tell either. They'd think the worse of you if you did.'

'This is silly. What's the point of having schoolmasters if they have no control over their boys?'

'They have control – but it's selective.'

'Hengrave Junior?' Dr Vincent appeared at the door, tapping his cane on his leg. 'Come in.'

Feeling like a prisoner walking to the gallows,

I entered his study. It was a warm, book-lined room with a view over the street outside. I could hear the carriages rattling by and the call of the hot chestnut seller in the Abbey Yard.

'Explain!' he barked.

'I slipped on some ice, sir,' I said quietly.

'Speak up! I'm not as young as I was.'

'I slipped on some ice, sir.'

He looked at me from under his bushy brows, a smile hovering on his lips. I realized that he knew exactly what had happened to me. 'That was very stupid of you.'

'Yes, sir.'

'Well, don't do it again or I'll have to flog you for your carelessness, understood?'

'Yes, sir.' That was the final absurdity. I was to be flogged if I got beaten up again. He knew I couldn't help it, but no matter.

'And I've written to your mother to tell her that you met with . . . with an accident that kept you off lessons for three days. Make sure you work hard to catch up.'

'My mother?' I croaked.

'Yes, boy. Who else do you expect me to write to? The Archbishop of Canterbury? Dismissed!'

I stumbled from the room and broke the news to Charlie: a letter was winging its way to Dublin to a bemused Lady Hengrave.

He grimaced. 'That gives us about a week, I'd say. Lord, Tom will be surprised to hear he's missed lessons before he even started them.'

Now the end of my stay in Westminster School had been sighted, I went up to my room to check the necessary items for my escape plan. Lizzie had been as good as her word: they were all there, waiting for the right occasion. The first sign of news from Ireland and Tom Cat would be gone.

Chops arrived on Friday night without us sending for them. Their bringer, Syd, had come to tell us how the search for Pedro was progressing. He also brought other, stranger news. But first he had to do what he usually did: take me to task like a big brother who always thinks he knows best. The prompt was seeing the fading bruises on my face.

'What's 'appened to you, Cat?' he said, pulling me closer as he made a quick inspection of all exposed areas of skin. 'Right, that's it. This ends 'ere and now. I'm takin' you back with me.'

'Back where, Syd?' I asked grimly. 'You're forgetting that if I go with you, I'll end up in gaol by tomorrow.'

He brushed this minor detail aside. 'You've been gettin' in fights, ain't you, Cat? I know you – you can't keep your temper five minutes. You let your big mouth run away with you. I should never've left you 'ere.'

'Cat's not been *picking* fights,' said Frank, leaping to my defence. 'She's being *picked* on. A gang of boys decided to kick her unconscious for their own amusement.'

Syd's reaction was predictable. I braced for the volcanic eruption that I knew would follow Frank's indiscreet remark.

'Where are they? Let me at 'em! Their own

mothers won't recognize them when I've finished.' He rounded on Frank. 'And where were you when our Cat was bein' done over, eh?' He took Frank by the lapels and pushed him up against the wall. I'd never seen Syd so angry. 'I trusted you to look after 'er!'

'Syd, listen,' I said, trying to pull him away, but I might as well have attempted to move a mountain. 'He was out searching for Pedro. He couldn't have done anything anyway. There were too many of them.'

Syd let go of Frank, still shaking with rage. Slowly, he began to calm down. 'Sorry, Frank. I got a bit carried away.'

'I understand, Syd,' said Frank, tucking in his shirt. He had the rumpled look of someone who had been out in a strong wind. 'I felt bad about it too when I got back. So did Charlie. They jumped her when she was on her own. But don't worry about them. We'll sort them out when the time's right.'

'Is that a promise?' asked Syd. Frank nodded.

'Let me know if me and the boys can 'elp.'

'I will.'

Syd turned to me and, with a hesitant gesture, stroked my hair. 'So are you all right, Cat?'

'I've been better but I'll live. The worst part is that the headmaster has written to Charlie's mother, so I have to find somewhere else to hide.'

Syd scratched his head. 'I could ask one of my boxin' chums if they could find a place for you.'

'Don't worry about me: I've got a plan.'

'Of course I worry about you, Cat. What do you expect? I s'pose you're not goin' to tell us what this plan of yours is?'

I smiled. 'How did you guess?'

'You 'ave a shifty look when you're tryin' to keep a secret. I've seen it before.' Syd had surprised me. I had always thought him a bit slow to notice these things. 'As long as it's not dangerous, I don't think I want to know.'

'No, it's not dangerous. In fact, I'm probably heading for the safest place in England.'

Syd gave me another appraising look then nodded. 'All right. I trust you. You always seem to land on your feet so I've no reason to think you won't this time.'

Charlie and Syd took this as the signal that Syd had calmed down and was safe to approach. Frank sat Syd in the best armchair, I took the footstool, while Charlie and Frank shared the bench which they dragged to the fireside.

'So what's the news about Pedro?' Frank asked.

'Well, that's the rum thing. It's why I come this evenin'. Joe finally caught up with Blind Bob this mornin' but only 'cos Bob 'ad a message for 'im. That fleabag, Billy Shepherd, wants to speak to me. 'E says 'e 'as information about our Prince. Boil's asked me to bring the boys to the Pantheon on Oxford Street tonight.'

'What? For a fight? But the Pantheon's a ballroom!' exclaimed Charlie.

Syd shook his head. 'Nah, not for a fight – not that we wouldn't be ready for one if 'e offers – but to talk – man to man, 'e said.' He leaned forward, lowering his voice. 'I've 'eard that the Pantheon's on the slide – no longer the place it was. Rumour 'as it that Shepherd bought a stake in it.'

'Don't tell me – he's expanding his operations westwards,' I said with a groan. 'And who said that crime doesn't pay? That'll be a big step up from ruling the roost in the Rookeries.'

'That's right, Cat. Shepherd's got a lot of money from somewhere lately – and he's been buyin' into businesses left, right and centre. Not in Covent Garden, of course.' Syd gave a proud smile. ''E 'asn't tried it on there, knowin' what I'd do to 'im if 'e put a foot into my patch.'

'And do you believe him – I mean, believe that he knows something about Pedro?'

Syd nodded. 'Stands to reason, don't it? I'd wager my next boxin' purse on Pedro still bein' in London. Shepherd might well know where 'e is.'

'So, you're going to meet him?'

'Course. Got the boys waitin' for me – we're

goin' in style. But there's just one thing that's botherin' me.'

'What's that?'

''E's asked me to bring you along too.' Syd sat back and looked at me, one eyebrow raised sceptically. 'What d'you think of that?'

I was as suspicious as he was. Shepherd hated my guts. 'It must be a trap.'

'That's what I thought, but Shepherd sent me this as proof 'e's straight.' Syd took out a leather bag from his pocket and placed it on the table. I opened the string and saw that it was full of guineas.

'There must be one hundred pounds in there!' I shook my head in disbelief.

'Yeah, Cat. It's a kind of ransom for you. If 'e tricks us, 'e forfeits this.'

Did Billy Shepherd hate me enough to lose a hundred pounds on me? I wondered. I doubted it. Billy loved money more than his own mother.

'And there's somethink else. 'E swore that 'e wouldn't tell us nothink unless you came to the meetin'.' Syd prodded the coins. 'What d'you think, Cat?'

'I don't know. I don't trust him.'

'Course not. 'E knows that.'

'She mustn't go,' said Frank quickly. 'It smells bad to me.'

'Stinks to 'igh 'eaven,' agreed Syd. 'But what about Prince? We'll 'ave all the boys there – we're more than a match for Shepherd's gang of squealers and any runners that 'e might invite along. We can get 'er away if there's trouble.'

I knew I didn't really have any choice – I would never forgive myself if we passed up this chance to find Pedro. Billy probably knew that too.

'Of course I'll come,' I said. 'Can I borrow your cloak, Frank?'

'But I'm coming as well,' he said.

'So am I,' declared Charlie.

'The more the merrier, as far as I'm concerned,' said Syd.

'But I still need a cloak – something to hide me from curious eyes.'

'My guess is,' said Syd, rubbing his chin, 'that's what this is all about. 'E knows you're in trouble and wants a chance to crow.'

Frank handed me his spare cloak.

'You may be right,' I said, throwing it on and pulling up the hood. 'And if I were him, I'd probably want the chance myself, seeing how we parted on such good terms when last we met.'

Syd's boys were lounging outside the Pantheon, waiting for their leader. The gang had grown since I last saw it gathered in one place. The ranks had been swelled by a score of heavily built, large-fisted individuals – chums from the boxing ring, Syd explained. I wondered how many of them had pledged their allegiance to my friend after being floored by his formidable right hook – quite a few from the evidence of their squashed noses.

Syd gave them a brief inspection. They were all turned out in their best as if ready for a night on the town. Syd brushed off the lapels of his own claret jacket – a new purchase in honour of the occasion, I guessed. Leading a gang was all about commanding respect. Syd did not want to fall short in his boys' eyes when meeting his rival. Though from the sound of it, Billy Shepherd was promoting himself into another league altogether, far from his roots in the small beer of controlling a market. Syd had been made the uncrowned king of Covent Garden because he was well liked by his fellow shopkeepers and stall-holders and trusted to exercise his own brand of rough justice in a reasonably fair manner. Billy had always been more interested in what he could get for himself and had been trusted by no one.

Nick, Syd's second in command, greeted me warmly before turning to Syd.

'The Boil's got a private room for the meetin'. We're to go in by the side entrance.'

This was just as well. I doubted that the footmen of the Pantheon would welcome a crowd of burly lads breaking in upon the night's entertainment. From the strains of the orchestra coming out of the grand pillared entrance, there appeared to be a ball or concert in progress.

'Right you are. Fall in, lads,' said Syd. I found myself surrounded by some of the biggest boys in the gang, sandwiched between them so that I was almost carried along off my feet. Syd had been serious in his promise to keep me safe.

The doorman let in the Butcher's Boys without a word, indicating that we should proceed up the carpeted stairs to the plush hall above. Bright candles in wall brackets lit our way, reflected from the tarnished gilt mirrors that covered the walls. It reminded me a little of the corridors of Drury Lane and I felt a pang of regret that I wasn't going home tonight. We marched up, like an invading army, and arrived outside a white-painted double door. Syd thumped once and the doors were thrown open. In spite of himself, he hesitated on the threshold, taken aback by what he saw before him. The room was like an enormous box in the theatre, except it looked out on a ballroom filled with couples, brilliant as butterflies, all dancing to the music of a full orchestra on a stage at the far end. The ballroom was circular with an ornate painted ceiling – the largest dome I'd seen outside of St Paul's. Rather than being deafened by the noise of the instruments, we heard the music as if from a great distance, thanks to the barrier provided by the glass-panelled doors that opened out on to a balcony.

'Lovely, ain't it?' said Billy Shepherd, stepping forward, his hand outstretched to Syd. He had filled out since I last saw him; he looked both older and more impressive. He wore a shiny purple jacket like a beetle's shell over immaculate white breeches. His dark hair was fashionably styled, tied back in a black bow, but his teeth were as rotten as ever and I was pleased to see that his boil had swelled on the end of his nose, despite his best efforts to improve his appearance. At eighteen, he was now in his prime. But if his rise had been meteoric, his fall was likely to be as swift. Gang leaders of his sort did not expect to live much beyond twenty unless they were extraordinarily lucky – if the law didn't get them, a rival would. In the poorer streets where I come from, everyone knows that if you make it to twenty-five, you're fortunate – thirty is positively ancient.

Syd looked at the hand Shepherd held out to him as if it were a pound of rotten offal before reluctantly shaking it. I glanced round quickly and counted twenty of Shepherd's boys, along with a few girls in gaudy dresses, who were lounging against the walls. We were the stronger party by far.

'Very pretty, Shepherd,' said Syd with the closest thing to a sneer I had ever heard him use.

'You see, Fletcher, I've gone up in the world since we last met.' With evident self-satisfaction, Billy gestured to his new empire.

'He means up from louse to cockroach, I suppose,' I said in a stage whisper, causing a splutter of laughter from my end of the room.

Shepherd spun round quickly and spotted me in the middle of my guard. He gave me his old familiar crocodile grin. 'So you did bring Cat after all. That's good. I was beginning to fear that I was goin' to 'ave to with'old my information. But we can't 'ave a lady standin' while we sit, can we, Fletcher? Won't you join us?' He gestured to a table with three chairs by the glass doors, set ready with wine glasses and a decanter. I looked to Syd, who gave me a nod, so I stepped forward to join them. Shepherd pulled out a chair with a flourish and waited for me to sit down. I did so, keeping my cloak wrapped tight around me. 'Wine?' Billy asked. 'I'll water it down for the little 'un if she can't take the strong stuff yet.'

'Nothing for me,' I said quickly. 'I'd rather drink Fleet ditch water than anything you have to offer. I just want to hear what you've got to say about Pedro.'

Shepherd appeared to be enjoying himself immensely despite, or maybe because of my rudeness. 'All in good time, my dear.' He poured

Syd and himself a large glass of claret. 'It's a treat to 'ear our Cat, again, ain't it, Syd? You must be missin' 'er silver tongue. My girls are all too afraid of me – no one gives me cheek like she does.' He raised his glass to me and drank deeply. Syd took a sip of his, wisely keeping quiet. Syd and I both knew that Shepherd would get to the point sooner or later.

Shepherd gestured to my cloak. 'You cold or somethink, Cat?'

'No.' Indeed, it was warm in here thanks to the fire roaring in the grate.

'Then let me take your cloak.'

'N-no!' I protested, but too late: he'd tugged on the hood and revealed my shaven head. The sight of it sent him into a peal of laughter.

'Wot you done to yourself, Cat?' He leaned closer so that I could smell his stale breath. 'Still got the curls wot you cut off? If you 'ave, I'll give you a shillin' for 'em for the wig-maker.'

'Go hang yourself, Boil,' I spat back. Syd tensed, gripping the stem of his glass so hard that it was in imminent danger of snapping.

Shepherd sat at his ease and wiped his eyes. 'No 'ard feelin's, Cat, but you look so queer, wot with that crop and them there bruises. Not been usin' 'er for a punchbag, 'ave you, Fletcher? I thought you were sweet on 'er. You've a strange way of showin' your affection. You'd've been better off stickin' with me, Kitten.'

The wine glass smashed and Syd got up abruptly.

'Just jokin', Fletcher, just jokin',' said Shepherd. 'You won't 'ear wot I've got to say about Blackie if you fly off the 'andle like that.'

Syd sat down, his face flushed. I too felt hot under the collar, but more because I didn't like Shepherd's teasing about Syd and me. Syd was like a big brother. I'd hate to think of him in any other light.

Shepherd grinned at us. 'That's better. Now, I asked you 'ere to tell you that your boy's all right – kept close but still in the land of the livin'.'

'Where is he?' I asked.

'Why are you tellin' us this?' said Syd at the same time. I realized at once that his was the more pertinent question.

Shepherd poured himself another glass. 'Well, for a start, I know that you won't be able to touch 'im where 'e is, so "why not?" I asked meself when I woke up this mornin'. Second, 'e's asked to see Cat. 'E wants to say goodbye.'

'What? I don't believe you!' I exclaimed.

'Ain't you the suspicious sort, Cat? Let me put it another way: I asked 'im if there was anyone 'e'd like to see afore 'e went and 'e said you. I don't s'pose 'e thought for one minute that I'd try and bring you to 'im – 'e 'as me down as an 'ard-'earted cove, but I've nothink against 'im personally and I don't 'old with slavery, so I thought, why not give 'im wot 'e wants?'

I didn't believe any of that. It was either a trap or he was merely amusing himself by playing us along. We couldn't even be sure that he had seen Pedro as he claimed.

'You're thinkin' that I'm spinnin' you a load

of moonshine, ain't you, Cat?' said Shepherd, tipping me a wink.

I didn't reply.

'Well, I've got somethink that'll convince even you.' He placed a pearl earring on the table. We all recognized it immediately as Pedro's. 'Perhaps you might like to give it back to 'im, Cat? Poor blighter won't 'ave much where 'e's goin'.'

'You'll take us to him,' said Syd, more as a command than a question.

'Very funny,' said Shepherd with a bark of laughter. 'Take you so that you can spring 'im from 'is hidin' place? I don't think so. Nah, I'll take Cat and no one else.'

'Out of the question,' said Frank suddenly, stepping forward from the ranks and laying a hand on my shoulder.

Shepherd leant back in his chair and squinted up at Frank. 'Eh, Cat, your lucky day, ain't it? You've got yourself another protector. I remember 'im – dressed as a soot last time we met. I'd say you've gone up in the world too since then, my lord.'

Frank glowered at him and tightened his grip.

'If I'd known then that you were a gent, I'd've finished you off there and then,' said Shepherd affably. 'But now we're to be friends, ain't we? I do you a good turn now, and maybe you'll get me a seat in the 'Ouse in a few years, eh?'

Frank ignored this – it wasn't worthy of a response.

'Cat's not goin' on 'er own,' said Syd.

'Course not, she'll be with me,' said Shepherd with a smile so wide you could count his rotten teeth. 'And I don't expect you to take my good behaviour on trust, Fletcher. You've got the money – and I'll throw in me gang too. You can cut the throats of the lot of 'em if she doesn't return by two in the mornin'.'

This announcement was met by much alarmed muttering from Shepherd's boys.

'Shut it, you lot,' he snarled. 'Nothink will 'appen to any of you 'cos I'll be back 'ere to finish my wine well before the deadline.'

I could tell he'd been planning this all along. That was the reason the meeting was on neutral ground, and that was why he'd asked Syd to bring all his men: he wanted to make sure we'd believe him. But what possible interest could he have in taking me to see Pedro? Then again, I asked myself, did his motives matter? If I could see Pedro, we'd surely be better off than we were at the moment?

'I'll go,' I said firmly, shaking off Frank's hand.

Syd was struggling with his desire to help Pedro and his instinct to protect me. 'Shepherd, you promise not to let anyone else 'arm 'er – not the law, not no one?'

'Promise.' Shepherd's eyes glittered mischievously.

'And you go unarmed?'

'Of course.' He stood up and emptied an assortment of knives and ugly-looking wires from his various pockets.

'Don't forget your boot,' I said, remembering

a particularly long night spent with him in the Bow Street lock-up.

Shepherd grinned at me and took out a long, thin blade from his boot and threw it on the table.

Frank seized Syd's arm. 'This is madness, Syd. You can't let her go with him. We'll never see her alive again!'

Shepherd looked directly at Syd. 'I give you me word that I'll not 'arm an 'air of 'er 'ead – not that she's got many of those left.'

'Why should we trust you?' Frank asked.

Shepherd shrugged. 'I'm not askin' you to trust me. You've got me money, me boys, even me own beloved knives – that's what you should trust, Dook.'

'We're not goin' to get any more from 'im, Frank,' said Syd. 'Either we let Cat go or we kiss goodbye to our chance to 'elp Prince.'

None of us liked it – me least of all – but Shepherd had us over a barrel.

'Oh, come on,' I said irritably, doing my best

to hide my fear, 'the sooner we go, the sooner I'll be back.'

Syd drew me aside while Shepherd donned his street clothes.

'Cat,' he whispered. 'Just in case.' And he pressed the thin blade Shepherd had removed from his boot into my hand. I nodded and slipped it inside my cloak. I prayed that I would not have to use it.

SCENE 3 – RATS' CASTLE

'Right then, Kitten, follow me!' declared Shepherd in great good humour.

'Don't call me Kitten,' I grumbled as I followed him down the stairs. 'Only my friends call me that.'

Shepherd laughed. 'But I am your friend, Kitten – for tonight anyways. We 'ave a score to settle, you and I, but it can wait for another day.'

'You may feel in a friendly humour, fine, but just don't call me Kitten.'

'All right, all right . . . Moggy.'

It was breathtakingly cold on the street after the warmth of the glass room. Shepherd kept up a fast pace, forcing me to trot beside him to keep up.

'You know, Moggy,' he said suddenly, coming to a halt outside a brightly lit tavern, 'I feel sorry for you.'

'What?' I panted.

'On the run, no 'ome, pretendin' to be a boy with your 'air and everythink – don't think I don't know why you done it. I could look after you, y'know.'

'Look after me? Oh yes, I know your kind of tender loving care. You'd lead me a merry dance, I've no doubt, ending with me cutting a caper on nothing when you sell me out to the Beak.'

'You've got me all wrong,' said Shepherd with mock sorrow. 'The last thing I want is to see you 'anged.'

'No, but that's only because it's the first thing you want.'

Shepherd gave a shout of laughter. 'You're no fool, Cat. I bet you'll die damned 'ard and bold as brass when your time comes on the platform. I look forward to it.'

I was too cold to have any appetite to continue this exchange. I just wanted to see Pedro. 'Look, Billy, did you drag me out here only to bait me?'

He shook his head. 'Nah, Moggy, we need to make a turn down 'ere.'

Shepherd led the way into a narrow alley that ran between the tavern and a warehouse. It was the kind of place I'd normally avoid like the plague as it headed into the Rookeries – the maze of crumbling houses and courtyards that had given Shepherd his start on the road to power and riches. I glanced around me before committing myself. A couple of men lounging outside the tavern were watching me, the light pouring from the window gilding their drab clothes with temporary splendour. I turned back. Shepherd's black cloak was disappearing into the darkness – I'd lose him if I didn't hurry.

'In for a penny, in for a pound,' I muttered, stealing myself to take the plunge.

I found him waiting for me at the other end of the alleyway. 'Stick close, Cat,' he said in a low voice, taking my elbow. 'You'll come to no 'arm as long as you're with me.'

I remembered my last visit to the Rookeries –

the night Shepherd tried to cut my throat. The smell was as rank, the streets as dirty, the buildings as crazed as they had been then. But there was one major change: no one approached us or tried to rob me. Instead, as we passed the beggars huddled on doorsteps, the men and women clustered in the doorways to the gin palaces and grotty taverns, they all stood to attention.

'Evenin', Mr Shepherd,' said one red-nosed Irishman, tipping his hat to my companion. A street-walker in a ragged petticoat dropped a curtsey.

Shepherd acknowledged their greetings with a slight nod of his head.

'You see, Cat, I'm all they've got. I'm king, judge and jury to 'em. I'm more of a ruler 'ere than King bleedin' George on his bleedin' throne. My word is life or death.'

And he was loving it, lapping up the signs of fearful respect his passage through the Rookeries was prompting from his unfortunate subjects. To command this kind of attention from the most hard-bitten and desperate of London's poor, he must have done some terrible things to them. I wondered how many he'd killed, how many businesses he'd done over, whom he'd bribed. It was then I understood what I was doing here: Billy was a born showman suffering from lack of an audience. He had arranged all this to impress me, his sworn enemy. Not that I was much of a threat to him: he knew he could swat me like a fly if he wanted. To send one of his boys after me on a dark night would be the work of a moment. But he wanted more than this: he wanted to convert me. He knew I despised him; he wanted me to admire him. Well, he could fling his cap after me – he'd come to the wrong person if he wanted even the most grudging esteem.

'Remember, Cat, I once offered you a share in all this?' he said with a sweep of his arm at his kingdom. 'Funny really, now I think about it. You're such a queer little thing, but there's some-think about you that . . . well, that . . .'as promise. You're like me: I started from nothink and now

I've got me foot on the first rung of the ladder to 'igh society.'

'Oh, please!' I snorted.

'You'll see,' said Shepherd, refusing to be offended by my scorn, 'money can buy a 'ell of a lot of blue blood. You got your claws into those Avons by your own nous, didn't you? You must be clever enough to understand 'ow it can be done.'

'You think I'm milking Frank and his family for money?'

'Well, ain't you?'

I was about to make a virulent denial, but then remembered the guineas Frank had had to shell out to cover my expenses at school. 'They're my friends,' I said lamely.

'They're the best kind of milk cow, Cat, as I'm sure you know.'

'How would you know, not having any friends to speak of?'

Shepherd came to a sudden stop. I thought for a moment that I had gone too far, but I was wrong.

'This is it, Moggy,' he announced.

I looked up. We were standing in front of a once fine building, a vast place with many windows and a pillared porch. It was surrounded by a high wall with an iron gate set in an archway. But the gracious elegance was all gone, replaced by boarded gaps where once had been glass, missing slates, and filth-smeared walls. 'This is Rats' Castle.'

I thought the place was just a legend. Rats' Castle was an old leper hospital, built by benevolent gentlemen in the days when the Rookeries had been a respectable part of town – a stylish dumping ground for those inflicted with severe skin diseases where they could rot away surrounded by opulence. It had fallen far and now seemed more like a leper victim itself, as if the ailments of its former inhabitants had transferred into the stones. No one had repaired the building for decades but they had added to it in a bizarre and haphazard fashion. The castle's old isolation had been breeched by rickety wooden walkways connecting it to the roofs of the neighbouring slums. Shacks had sprouted on the slates and against the walls like fungi on a rotting trunk, giving shelter to hundreds of people.

'That's where we're goin',' said Shepherd, thumbing towards a ladder leaning against the wall. It connected to one of the highest walkways. 'Are you game for the jaunt, Moggy?'

'All right,' I said, feeling my mouth go dry.

'But I'll have to blindfold you.' He pulled a blue silk handkerchief from his pocket like a conjuror. 'There are certain secrets about this place I don't want you to see.'

'You can't be serious?'

'It's clean – well, quite clean,' said Shepherd, giving the handkerchief a sniff.

'I don't mean the wipe – you want me to walk across there blind?'

'Yeah. Why? Is that a problem, Miss Royal?'

'Of course it's a problem, you idiot! I'll kill myself.'

'Nah you won't. I'll be guidin' you. You'll just have to trust me.'

'But I don't . . .'

'Trust me,' he finished. 'I know. But it's part of the fun. Why do you think I'm doin' this if not to make you sweat a little?'

'Boil, you are the biggest pile of dung ever produced by a pox-ridden, fart-filled cow,' I fumed as he tied the handkerchief around my eyes.

'You're just sayin' that 'cause you love me so much,' he said. Even with my eyes bound, I was sure he was grinning. 'Come on, 'old me 'and.' He took me to the ladder and curled my fingers around the bottom rung. 'Now climb till I say stop.'

I did as I was told, trying not to think about the many tricks he could play on me in this situation. Did he think he could get away with telling Syd that I'd fallen by accident? Surely not: he'd know Syd would blame him for anything that happened to me.

'Right, Moggy, stop there.' I could feel a cold breeze on my face as if we were high up above the level of the surrounding buildings. 'If you reach in front of you, you'll find a platform. Step on to it.' It was as he said. I stood on the boards not daring to move. I doubted there would be a rail to catch me if I strayed. 'Take me 'and. This time I go first.'

'You think your scaring me, don't you, Boil,' I said, more to keep my spirits up than anything as we edged along the walkway. 'Well, you're wrong.'

'Oh, am I?' he said archly. 'Then you won't mind if I let go of your 'and then?' He pulled himself free of my grip. 'And wot if I jump up and down a bit to keep warm?' His boots thumped on the planks, making the whole walkway judder. I staggered, arms flailing. 'Oh, and mind the 'ole in front of you.' I gave a shriek and threw myself in the direction of his voice, catching hold of his legs as my foot fell through into nothingness. 'Still not scared, Cat?' he asked as he put his arms around me to haul me back to my feet. 'So why are you shakin' like a leaf, eh?'

I pushed him away. 'Don't, Billy! Don't do

that again.' But there was no point in pleading with someone as ruthless as him.

'Don't do wot? This?' He began to jump again. The walkway groaned and creaked.

There was only one thing for it. I pushed past him and set off unaided across the planks.

'Wot you doin', you daft cow?' he called after me. I stomped on. If I fell, it was his gold, his gang that he would forfeit. I guessed he was not going to lose all that if he could help it. The jumping stopped and he swiftly took my arm again.

'I say one thing for you, Cat: you've got more pluck than all me boys put together,' he said hoarsely. 'Almost there now.'

The feeling of the air changed as we entered the building. It smelt damp and foul as if rubbish had accumulated here for years and festered where it lay. Shepherd turned me round a few times then took off my blindfold. I couldn't see exactly what part of the building we were in because all the windows were boarded. The only light came from a lantern swinging from a hook in the ceiling. Plaster hung loosely from the walls like trailing bandages, giving a glimpse of dark rooms beyond.

'Where's Pedro?' I asked. This room was empty, apart from two wooden chairs and a table.

'I told you 'e was bein' kept close,' said Shepherd, going to an iron ring set in the floor and pulling on it. With a creak, he raised the trapdoor to reveal a windowless hole in the belly of this rotting corpse of a house.

'Who's there?' a faint voice called up from inside.

'Pedro!' I cried, rushing to the edge of the cavity.

'Is that you, Cat? Have you come to get me out?' Pedro asked, his voice full of hope.

'Nah, Blackie,' Shepherd called out cheerfully. 'But she can come down and visit you if she wants.' He took a ladder that was leaning against a wall and lowered it into the hole. 'Off you go, Cat. Give a whistle when you want to come up.' He handed me the lantern and settled himself down at the table, conjuring up a bottle from the pockets of his jacket to keep him company.

I'd come this far: I had to go the last few steps even if they were into a pit no bigger than a cupboard and darker than a moonless night. I could touch the damp walls with my arms outstretched – it was frighteningly like being trapped in a chimney flue. I'd heard of sweeps who had got stuck and suffocated in the dark: it had always been one of my worst nightmares to imagine their suffering. Biting down hard on my fear, I descended the ladder and held up my lantern. Pedro was sitting on the edge of a mattress, empty plate and bottle by his side, staring at me in amazement.

I put the lantern on the floor and hugged him. 'It's so good to see you again, Pedro,' I said, half-sobbing.

Pedro pulled away. 'Have they caught you too?' he asked fearfully.

'No. Shepherd brought me here.'

'Why?'

'No idea. He said you asked to see me.'

'I did – but I thought he was joking when he said he'd bring you. He's been quite decent really.' Pedro looked down at the floor. He seemed different somehow – resigned, crushed, weighed down by the memories of the past. 'He talks to me when he's got the time, makes sure I have enough food and water. He's told the boys who guard me not to hurt me.'

That put a new complexion on things.

'I didn't realize,' I said softly.

'Didn't realize what?'

'That he's your gaoler.'

'Of course. My master's paid him to keep me here – like he paid that piano tuner to snatch me from the house.'

'Your *old* master, Pedro,' I corrected him, worried by this new turn of phrase.

Pedro said nothing, but he let go of my hand.

'What's going to happen to you? Do you know?' I asked, trying to be practical.

'They're taking me to Jamaica, they say.

That's if I don't manage to kill myself first, of course.' He gave me a bitter smile. 'I tried to throw myself off that wooden bridge up there but they caught me. That's why I'm down here.'

I'd contemplated giving Pedro the knife but this changed my mind. If I couldn't get him out of here tonight, I certainly wasn't going to leave him alone with it.

'Look, Pedro, it's only Shepherd up there at the moment. He's unarmed. Why don't we try and make a run for it?' I whispered.

'No,' he said.

'Why not?' I asked, beginning to feel annoyed by his defeatism. 'If we're quick enough up the ladder, we can overpower him and escape.'

'This is why.' He pointed to his neck. I lifted the lantern and saw that he was wearing an iron collar attached by a chain to the wall.

'Oh, Pedro!' I couldn't help it: I began to cry. All that I had been through over the last few weeks, all that Pedro was suffering, came out in a storm of tears. I buried my head on his shoulder.

He held me tight, offering comfort when it was him that needed it most.

'You mustn't worry about me, Cat,' he said bravely. 'It won't be so bad. I'll find a way out in the end. They can't watch me forever.'

'We'll help you,' I said, furious with myself. I wiped my eyes on my cloak. 'Mr Sharp knows how to stop you being taken against your will.'

'He has to find me first,' said Pedro grimly.

'And we will. I know where you are now. That's got to help. You mustn't give up hope.' I couldn't leave him like this. I wished I could give him something to remind him that he had friends. Of course! 'Have this.' I pressed the pottery medallion into his hand. 'And you should take this back too.' I threaded the pearl earring through his lobe. 'It's a sign of your freedom, Pedro – of your talent and your success.'

Pedro gripped the medallion hard and then touched his earring back in its old familiar place. 'Thank you, Cat. I'm going to miss you.'

'Not for long, because we'll both be back home soon.'

'Home?' he asked wistfully.

'Drury Lane, of course.' I sat back next to him, arm against arm, looking up at the open trapdoor. 'Theatre Royal, Drury Lane.'

'Well, well, well! If it ain't the little gal herself, flown right into the net.' I gave a scream as Kingston Hawkins' head appeared in the black square above us. 'Ain't that just dandy.'

'Careful, Cat!' hissed Pedro as I scaled the ladder as fast as I could, anger at being trapped running red hot through my veins.

'Boil, you lying toad!' I yelled, sure that this had all been part of his grand plan for the night.

Hawkins raised his foot to kick me back down the ladder but he was hauled back by Shepherd.

'Not the girl, sir,' he said. 'You can't 'ave Cat.'

'But . . .!' spluttered Hawkins in surprise.

'Our agreement is for the boy only. The girl's my business.'

I emerged out into the room and found Shepherd and Hawkins glaring at each other either side of the table. I didn't know which one I hated most. I flew at Hawkins, hitting out with feet and hands in a fury.

'You beast! I hope your own slaves chop you to pieces and feed you to your dogs. You evil pile of –'

I was pulled off him by a strong pair of arms, a blue handkerchief forced into my mouth to cut off my torrent of abuse.

'Leave it, Cat,' said Shepherd, increasing his grip on me as I struggled. 'I can't 'ave you abusin' a client.'

'So, Shepherd, this is how you repay my investment in you,' said Hawkins coldly as he brushed himself down.

'Wot I do 'ere is none of your business, Mr 'Awkins,' said Shepherd. 'As long as the boy's delivered safe and sound, wot do you care? Anyway, why you come 'ere? I told you it's not safe.'

'I'm just checking on the merchandise.'

''E's in top condition, ready to go whenever you say the word.'

'But the brat knows where he is now.'

'That's no matter. I was thinkin' of movin' 'im somewhere else. Somewhere she'll never find 'im.'

'But I've a score to settle with her.' Hawkins flexed his fist, which I was pleased to see was still bandaged. I shrank back closer to Shepherd, preferring the devil I knew to the one I didn't.

'Not till after I've delivered 'er back to her friends tonight. I've pledged me word not to 'arm 'er,' said Shepherd. 'After that, good luck to you, sir. But I should warn you: our Cat 'ere has the knack of gettin' out of tight corners. I'd put my money on 'er rather than you.'

'Then to hell with your word. I'll do for her now!' With a bone-chilling scrape, Hawkins drew a sword from his cane and brought it whistling down towards my throat. Shepherd thrust his hand into the pocket of my cloak and pulled out the blade Syd had given me, bringing it up still caught in the folds of cloth, to block the downstroke.

He'd known I had the knife all along.

'Now, Mr 'Awkins,' said Shepherd menacingly, 'don't get me angry. I've said no and I mean no.'

Hawkins took a step back and cut the air with his swordstick. 'Remember who's paying you, Shepherd.'

'For the boy only.'

'But what are you going to do against this?' Hawkins flourished the evil-looking blade. 'Your six inches of steel ain't goin' to stop this for long.'

'This is wot I'll do,' said Shepherd. So quickly I missed the flick, he hurled the knife across the room. It struck the corner of Hawkins' hat and clattered to the floor in the shadows.

'That wasn't very wise – you didn't hurt me and now you've lost your weapon.'

'I wasn't tryin' to 'it you, 'Awkins – if I 'ad, you wouldn't still be talkin'. As for losing my blade, I've got plenty more where that beauty came from.' With a strange movement of his wrist, a second knife appeared in front of me from up Shepherd's sleeve. 'Been throwin' blades since I was a nipper. Do you still want to argue over the girl? Like I said, nobody kills Cat except me – and tonight she's my guest.'

A small vein throbbed in Hawkins' temple, beating out his fury. I could see a succession of thoughts pass across his face. He realized his chances were slim: he was in the centre of Shepherd's empire and had just been given proof of the skills that brought his associate to be the cock on top of this particular dungheap. He decided to make light of it.

'Have it your way, Shepherd.' He replaced the sword in his cane with a clunk. 'If it *is* you that has the pleasure of cutting short her miserable life, I just hope you make the end long and painful.'

'I'll see wot I can do, sir.' Shepherd released his grip on me and vanished his knife up his sleeve again.

'I s'pose you don't have any objection to me inspecting my goods?'

Shepherd took off my gag. "'Elp yourself, sir.'
Hawkins moved to the head of the ladder. 'Why
don't you 'ave a little friendly chat with 'im while
you wait 'ere for me? I've got to take the girl
back. We can discuss further arrangements when
I return.'

I did not want to imagine Pedro's feelings
as he saw his old master descending into his
cell. I couldn't stop myself. 'Please, don't hurt
him!' I pleaded.

Hawkins paused, his head now level with the
floor. He gave me a wicked grin. 'I hadn't been
planning to, but now you've asked . . .'

I turned away so he wouldn't see my expression. I hated him – every foul inch of his body. I
wanted to stamp on him, crush him, but there
was nothing I could do.

'Let's go, Billy,' I said. 'I can't bear being in
the same room as him any longer.'

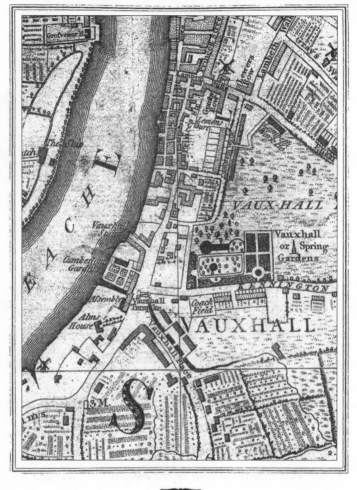

*Act IV – In which our heroine gives
an 'electra-fying' performance . . .*

ACT IV

SCENE 1 – ELECTRA-FYING

'Wot's the matter, Moggy? You're very quiet. Cat got your tongue?' Shepherd laughed as he steered me back through the alleyways.

I knew he wouldn't understand what it was like to leave a friend in trouble. He wouldn't be able to comprehend even a minute fraction of the torrent of emotion that was sweeping through me – none of my fear, anger and anxiety.

'You won't let him hurt Pedro, will you, Billy?' I asked, knowing it was useless, but I had to try something.

'None of my business wot 'e does with 'is boy, Moggy.'

'But Pedro isn't his boy. He's his own master.'

'There's few of us can say that. Anyways, that's all too deep for me. I'm doin' a job – that's all.'

'Well, in that case, couldn't we buy Pedro

from you? I'm sure we can pay more than Hawkins is giving you for the job, as you call it.'

Shepherd slapped me on the back and chuckled. 'Now you're thinkin' like me, Cat. But no thanks. I 'ave me name to protect among the cantin' crew. If they knew I'd double-crossed a client, me reputation would be mud.'

'It's a strange time to discover morality, Billy,' I muttered angrily.

'It's not morality: it's business.' The clock in St Giles struck the quarter. 'We'd better get our skates on, Moggy. I don't want your Syd nickin' me knives for bein' a few minutes late.'

It had been a strange, terrible night. I felt exhausted and could hardly keep up with Shepherd as he walked briskly back towards the Pantheon. My boots rubbed and my toes were frozen. Tripping on a broken paving stone, I fell on all fours into a foul-smelling puddle. Shepherd turned and watched me stagger back to my feet. He was smiling.

'I 'ope you enjoyed our little jaunt together,'

he said as I wiped the mud off my hands. 'I 'ave. I'll say one thing for you, there's never a dull moment when you're around, wot with everyone who meets you wantin' to kill you.'

'I s'pose I should thank you for stopping Hawkins from running me through,' I said grudgingly.

'Nah, don't do that. I only did it 'cos I didn't want 'im to deny me the pleasure of killin' you meself one day. For now, you make me laugh, but when I've 'ad enough of that, I'll make sure there's somethink special in store for you.' His stare was chilling, like a snake biding its time before the strike. I couldn't understand why he took such a malign interest in me; surely I wasn't worth it? I was a scruffy orphan with no stake in anything; he a gang leader with a growing empire. 'Somethink slow and painful like Mr 'Awkins said. No quick knife in the ribs for you.'

'Thanks. I look forward to it,' I replied sardonically. It was a strange moment as we both knew he was joking in deadly earnest. His behaviour made no sense.

We reached the Pantheon with five minutes to spare. Stopping by the back entrance, I caught his arm.

'Tell me one thing, Billy, before we get back to Syd and the others. Why do you bother with me? I can't believe that I'm so important to you that you'd risk annoying a client, but you did that for me tonight.'

He looked down at my hand then covered it with his, drawing me closer.

'You know the answer, Cat,' he hissed in my ear. His whisper made my skin crawl. 'You turned me down and I don't like that. I can 'ave anythink I want now – fine clothes, a flash 'ouse, a carriage or two – but I still can't 'ave you, can I? You won't join me gang, so I thinks, if I can't 'ave 'er, I'll kill 'er – but not just yet.'

There wasn't anything I could say to that. His eyes were burning a hole through me, so hate-filled was his stare. Or was it something else? Whatever it was, I didn't like what I saw. I pulled away.

'Come on, or Syd'll be practising his butchery on your boys.'

I ran up the stairs, feeling as if I had just escaped falling into a pit even deeper than the one in which Pedro now lay.

The freezing fog over the Thames was flushed pink with the dawn when Syd delivered us back to Westminster School. The porter said nothing as we slipped inside, thanks to the coin that Frank palmed him.

'I'll send the account very soon, my lord,' said Syd loudly for the porter's benefit. He added in a softer voice to me, 'I'm goin' to work out 'ow we can spring Prince from 'is trap, Cat. I gave 'im a promise and I intend to keep it, come 'ell or 'igh water.'

I gave him a miserable nod. 'Shepherd's web's hard to cut through. I don't fancy your chances in the Rookeries, not even with all your boys by your side.'

'Nah, that's not a fight I'd pick either,' agreed Syd. 'But Pedro can't stay in there forever. The river's the weak thread. We'll just 'ave to be ready. And thanks to you, we know that 'e's alive and well – that counts for a lot.' He patted my hand, turned and walked off whistling into the mist.

Frank ushered me up the staircase. 'You get some rest this morning, Cat. Charlie'll say you're ill.'

'Where are you going?' I asked, seeing that he was not following us up the stairs.

'I'm going to tell Mr Sharp and Mr Equiano what's happened. Charlie, let Dr Vincent know that Great-Aunt Charlotte's taken a turn for the worse.'

'But she died a couple of weeks ago, remember?' Charlie said.

'Oh yes.' Frank scratched the back of his head. 'Well, her twin sister is pining since her loss and not likely to live long.'

'And that's Great-Aunt – ?'

'Eugenia.'

'Got it,' Charlie said with a grin.

'And you expect me to sleep after all that?' I asked incredulously.

'Especially after "all that",' Frank confirmed. 'Don't you think you've put yourself through enough tonight? And, Lord knows, this week looks as though it might be an exciting one. Sleep – that's an order.'

'You can't tell me what to do,' I said, a shade resentfully. Shepherd's insinuations still rankled. I thought for a mad moment that Frank was parading his superior status before me, reminding me that I was only there because he was paying for me, that he owned me in some sense.

'Oh yes, I can.'

'Or what?' I challenged him.

'Or I'll set my mother on you.' Frank smiled and dispelled the illusion: it was just Frank being Frank, trying to look after me. 'You really don't want her to take you under her wing. Her pick-me-up potions are not recommended – she has a firm belief in experimenting with traditional medicine.'

'Witchcraft, you mean,' amended Charlie.

'Unconventional herbal remedies is a politer way of putting it,' said Frank.

'Point taken,' I said submissively. 'I'll go to bed.'

I woke up late in the afternoon to hear the boys talking in soft voices. Wrapping Frank's dressing gown around me, I padded barefooted out to the study to hear the news.

'What did Mr Sharp say?' I asked eagerly. 'Is there anything to be done for Pedro?'

Frank had a piece of bread on the end of a toasting fork and was holding it over the flames.

'Honey or jam?' he asked. That meant it was bad news.

'Spit it out, Frank. What did he say?'

Charlie got out of the armchair and handed me into it. Very bad news then.

'He said that we can't do anything even if we know where Pedro is and who has him,' said Frank heavily.

'Why not? Can't he use this habeas thingy?'

'*Habeas corpus*. No, because he would have to apply to the magistrate for it.'

'So?'

'The magistrate will say, "What proof do you have, sir, that Mr Hawkins, that respected businessman and donor to many worthy causes, is hiding this boy from us when he swears he doesn't know where he is?"'

'But we've seen him there. We know he's got him,' I protested.

'*You've* seen him there. *You* know he's got him.'

I realized what Frank meant. Mr Sharp could produce no witness because I was in hiding from the very same magistrate. Even if I did come forward, it would be my word against Hawkins and we all knew which side the law would come down on. Shepherd knew I could do nothing with the information he had given me.

'I hate Billy Shepherd,' I said fiercely, clenching my fists on the arms of the chair.

Frank looked at me strangely. 'He takes an

uncommon amount of interest in you, doesn't he? It's not healthy, Cat. I wouldn't encourage him.'

'Encourage him? You think I encourage him?' I asked, not believing I was hearing this.

'You answer him back, you make fun of him, you show you're not scared of him – need I say more?'

I was angry with Frank now. 'And you think this adds up to me encouraging him?' I rounded on Charlie. 'Do you think I encourage his . . . his attentions, Charlie?'

Charlie looked embarrassed and shrugged. 'It did strike me that you and Shepherd seemed to understand each other rather better than the rest of us did,' he offered.

'But I was just being me! I don't want a dog-breathed bully like Billy Boil to walk all over me!'

'Exactly,' said Frank, passing me the toast. 'That's why he likes you.'

'Likes me!' I was now incandescent with rage. 'He wants to kill me, you idiot – very slowly and painfully, he told me. It was only because Syd had his blessed knives that I'm still alive now!' I got up and threw the toast on the hearth. 'I'm not hungry.'

Slamming the door to my room, I sat with my back to it, head in my hands. Not meaning to eavesdrop, I heard Charlie say, 'She can't help it, Frank. She's not going to become a simpering female just to put Shepherd off.'

'But he loves manipulating her – it's like a game to him. He knows he can rely on her temper to make the sparks fly.'

'Are you saying you want Cat to change? To become like all those awful drawing-room misses we have inflicted on us when we go visiting?'

'Perish the thought, no! I wouldn't have her any other way. But she's making life very difficult for herself as she is. She said it: she's a magnet for trouble and unless she turns off the magnetism, she's going to keep on attracting Shepherd to her and one day . . .'

He didn't complete the sentence but I did it for him in my head. And one day, as he promised, Billy would simplify whatever it was he felt for me by killing the cat.

There was a buzz of excitement in the air as we filed into the Lower Form classroom on Monday morning. I'd missed so many lessons the previous week, I appeared to be the only one not in the know.

'How are you feeling, Hengrave?' asked Richmond with mock concern. 'Got over your fall yet?'

My mind filled with the humiliating memory of him rubbing my face in the dirt but I reined in my temper. I could take revenge another way.

'My meeting with the stones merely impressed on me how impoverished in wit and honour you and your friends are,' I said with a sweet smile in my best drawing room manner, though my words were laden with insult. If Frank wanted me to act like an insipid miss, then that's what he'd get and we'd see if he liked it. Richmond was disconcerted – as well he might be, for I knew I looked my most girlish with this expression on my face. 'And I thank you for enlightening me.' I tipped my head to one side, finger pressed lightly to my cheek coquettishly. 'I also hadn't realized such small-brained thugs could walk and talk at the same time – that too was a revelation. Tell me, do you get the ape in you from your mother's or your father's side of the family?'

The boys on my bench laughed.

'Why, you little . . .' snarled Richmond.

Mr Castleton walked into the room, positively bursting with his news.

'Settle down, boys,' he said, giving us all an indulgent smile. 'Here it is: the cast of this year's Latin play!' He waved a piece of parchment in the air.

Checking his paper, he wrote a list of names up on the board. I heaved a sigh of relief – mine was not among the principal characters. I'd been worried that Mr Castleton's admiration of my reading skills would propel me into the limelight at the biggest social event of the school calendar. 'That's it for the men,' he said, stepping back. 'But this play is really about the women of Greece, about the loyalty of a sister to her fallen brother, so those of you chosen for these parts should not be ashamed.' My heart sank. I knew what was coming. And I was right. I was to play the lead, Electra.

'And I have some more news for you all,' Mr Castleton continued. 'We have a very special guest attending our first rehearsal this afternoon: His Royal Highness, the Prince of Wales. As old boys will know, he takes a keen interest in the play and has seen several of our productions. He's sent word that he's bringing Mr Sheridan, the great playwright himself, to give our young actors some tips.' A murmur of enthusiasm swept across the room. But my heart was in my boots. 'So we want to have an "electra-fying" performance, don't we, to impress our guests?' Mr Castleton's eyes rested on me.

'Yes, sir,' we intoned.

Electrifying it would be. I couldn't imagine what Mr Sheridan would think seeing me cavorting on the stage at Westminster School, pretending to be a boy cast as a girl. It would certainly send a few sparks through his system.

'You'll spend the lesson looking over your parts. Any questions?'

How quickly can I make a run for it? was the thought uppermost in my mind, but I had to sit it out till the end of the lesson. My attempt to leave on the bell was ruined by Mr Castleton.

'Hengrave, a word.'

I walked reluctantly to the front of the class. Fatty Ingels pushed roughly past me but Mr Castleton steadied me before I toppled over.

'About last week,' he began. 'You don't think what happened will mar your performance, do you? Are you quite recovered?'

He was just worried about his damned play. Where had I seen that obsession about the stage before? Oh yes, I remembered: backstage at Drury Lane. I smiled.

'I'm fine, sir.'

'Good, good. Then come with me now. I want to present you to our guests before the rehearsal so they can meet our new young star.'

'No!' I gave a strangled cry.

'Don't be silly, boy. They won't eat you.' Mr Castleton seized my arm, ignoring all the excuses I stammered out, and towed me over to the headmaster's office. He knocked respectfully on the door.

'Come!' bellowed Dr Vincent.

Mr Castleton, still gripping me firmly by the elbow, entered the room and gave a low bow to the assembled company. I bowed too, keeping myself hidden by the door. The Prince of Wales stood in the centre of the room, dressed in a holly berry red jacket, shiny black boots and snowy white shirt loaded with so much lace that his small head looked like a raisin floating on whipped cream.

'So is this the promising young actor you mentioned, Castleton?' said Prince George. 'We were telling Sherry here –' he waved to his left 'that you could certainly do with an injection of talent. Last year's female lead had a broken voice that squeaked like a battered old organ and he looked like the organ grinder's monkey too.'

Everyone but me laughed. I could not see Mr Sheridan yet – the door still shielded me – but I could hear his rich chuckle blending with the other gentlemen. It wouldn't be long now.

'Yes, this is he, your highness.' Mr Castleton gave me a firm shove in the back and I was propelled further into the room. I gave a low bow. What else could I do? Mr Sheridan gasped, then went into a violent coughing fit.

'You all right, Sherry?' asked the prince with concern.

'A glass of wine, Mr Sheridan?' offered Dr Vincent, hastily filling one of his best glasses with his finest vintage.

'I'll say "yes" for him, headmaster,' said the prince. 'After all, he never says "no".'

Mr Sheridan's coughing fit subsiding, the

prince turned back to me. 'The boy will certainly look the part, but can he act?' he asked Mr Castleton.

'Oh yes, sir. He's only been with us for a short time but he reads with such passion and sense – it's a joy to hear.'

My eyes slid to Mr Sheridan. It was some relief to know that he hadn't shouted out my true identity the moment he saw me. His eyes were on me, an expression of – what was it? – of pride in them? I risked a quizzical look. He gave me a slight nod.

'So, boy, how did you learn to act so well?' the prince asked me.

'I had some very good teachers, your highness,' I said, glancing back at Mr Sheridan. He now gave me a broad smile.

'Where are you from, boy?'

'From Dru –, from Dublin,' I amended.

'He's one of the Hengraves from Leinster, your highness,' said Dr Vincent, picking up a letter from the top of the pile on his desk and

waving it. 'You may remember his mother –
Lady Ann Hengrave. She was a lady-in-waiting
to your mother before her marriage.'

The Prince of Wales nodded vaguely. Clearly
he did not spend much time thinking about his
mother's household. My thoughts were far from
vague, however, as my eyes fixed on the envelope
in Dr Vincent's hand: the letter had arrived, but
the seal was not yet broken. Time for Tom Cat to
hop the twig.

But I had not reckoned on Mr Sheridan having a bit of fun with me now he had recovered
from his surprise.

'So, young Hengrave,' he said the name with
relish, 'what kind of roles do see yourself most
suited to?'

'Feste, sir – the fool,' I replied quickly.

'What about Viola? Or Rosalind? Or Portia?'
He'd named all the most famous breeches roles
in Shakespeare.

'Oh no. Perhaps Brutus in *Julius Caesar*.'

'Whatever for?' asked Mr Sheridan, grinning

at me as he sensed what was coming.

'He gets to stab his patron in the back when the patron proves too annoying.'

'Very good,' chuckled Sheridan. 'I'll remember that when we next meet, young Hengrave.'

'Poppycock, Sherry,' said the prince, snapping his fingers. 'The child can't play Brutus. You stick to the women's parts while you're young, boy. You won't be able to play them when you sprout a beard, you know.'

'In that case, I'll take your advice, sir. I don't think I'm quite ready for a beard.'

The prince waved me away with his chubby hand. Mr Sheridan gave a wink and drained his glass to me. I made another bow and darted from the room, running all the way back to my staircase without pausing to catch my breath. I didn't have a moment to lose.

Abracadabra: Thomas Hengrave was about to disappear.

SCENE 2 – OLD JEAN'S BEAGLES

I wasn't quite quick enough. I had calculated that the headmaster would be spending the hours until the rehearsal escorting his royal guest, but I was wrong. He had returned to his paperwork far sooner than I had imagined. I had written a farewell letter, changed and packed a few belongings in a bundle but not yet left the room when an almighty commotion broke out in the courtyard below. I peered out the window. Dr Vincent was standing in the middle of the Dean's Yard and bellowing, 'Hengrave! Hengrave Junior and Senior, my office, now!' When neither of us emerged to obey his summons, he shouted to a passing boy. 'You there! Fetch the Hengraves!'

There was no time to get down the stairs unnoticed. Footsteps could be heard coming up to fetch me. I hid my bundle in the coal scuttle, blackened my hands and face with ash and knelt on the hearth. A boy burst into the room. As my luck would have it, it was Ingels. He was confronted by the sight of the scullery maid in demure close-fitting cap, laying the fire.

'Oi you! Have you seen Thomas Hengrave? He's a little squirt with red hair who lives in these rooms,' Ingels said rudely.

I got up, wiped my nose on the back of my hand and bobbed a curtsey, keeping my eyes lowered. 'Nah, sir, I ain't seen no one since I came up 'ere. I think 'e went skatin' on the duck pond.' This was the furthest point of the school from here.

I was fortunate that I had been interrupted by one of the densest pupils in my class. It did not occur to him to ask himself what a change of clothes might do for a person.

'If he comes back, tell him he's wanted by the headmaster.'

'Yes, sir.' I bobbed another curtsey.

Ingels left quickly. For the first time, I thanked Dr Vincent for his reputation as a flogger: he would not hesitate to blame Ingels for failing to find the Hengraves soon enough so the boy was in a hurry to execute his errand.

I risked another peek outside. I had to get out of here in case someone more penetrating than Ingels should come looking for me, but the quad was now full of pupils. Everyone knew something serious was up. Footsteps again and I slipped behind the door.

'Cat?' Frank whispered urgently. I came out of my hiding place and he did a double take. 'That's good,' he said. 'That's uncommonly good.' He nodded with approval at my plain grey dress, coarse apron, clogs and severe cap: I looked like the most downtrodden maid of all work, thanks to Lizzie's gifts.

'There's a letter on the table that should help you both,' I said, grabbing my bundle and shawl. 'I've got to get out but there's so many people about I'm afraid someone will spot me.'

Frank picked up the letter and read it quickly.

'Cat, you're a marvel. This might just save Charlie from expulsion. He expects a thrashing, of course – we can't do anything about that. He's hiding in the library looking studious and innocent.'

I was rather proud of the letter. The idea for it had come to me while being grilled on my origins in the presence of Mr Sheridan, the Irish actor turned statesman.

Dear Charlie

I apologize for working such a deception on you. As you will know by now, I am not in fact your younger brother, Thomas, as I claimed. My parents are actors and they placed me with the same tutor in Dublin as your brother. I knew that he was due to attend Westminster School, that he had been ill and that you his older brother had not seen him for many months. By studying his behaviour carefully and learning all that I could about your family, I thought to try my fortune by passing myself off as him, claiming to be much wasted by disease. To this end, I forged a letter from your gracious mother to the headmaster, having had the pleasure of seeing her hand many times while studying with the real Thomas Hengrave. I admit that I had a wager on the outcome with some friends at the theatre, which explains my motives.

Please pass on my regrets to Mr Castleton that I will be unable to accept the role of Electra. As a man of great perception, he was the first to sense my theatrical background and I have no doubt that the clever teachers at Westminster School would have soon smoked me out. (There was no harm in laying on the flattery so that they wouldn't feel so stupid).

I know that you will feel angry now, but perhaps in time you will forgive me. I hope the guineas you have spent on me will be thought punishment enough and teach you to be more suspicious.

With the money I have earned on my wager I am bound for India to join my uncle in the Hussars so do not try to trace me – I will be gone.

Yours in haste,

Thomas Bennington-Smythe.

Frank put the letter in his pocket. 'Well this is another scrape, Cat, and no mistake: the quad is teeming with boys; Dr Vincent is on the warpath; the heir to the throne and your patron are both about the place. How are we going to get away with it this time, even in your woman's weeds?' But for all his words of doom, he was grinning – highly delighted by the absurdity of the situation.

I wasn't as amused as he: the consequences of being caught out as a girl were too horrible to be imagined.

'I just need a few minutes to slip across the quad and past the porter. We need a diversion . . .'

Frank tapped his temple. 'I have the perfect idea – kill two birds with one stone.'

'What?'

'Revenge, Cat. Charlie and I have been recruiting chaps of the right sort to take our revenge on the planters' boys for their attack on you. Mouthy Southey and the others are all up

for it, just waiting for the opportune moment –
and this is it. Give me five minutes and there'll be
a distraction such as you've never seen before.'

'Frank, you're not to get in trouble for my sake.'

'Oh, you're a fine one to speak, Miss Never-
get-into-any-trouble-for-a-friend Royal.'

I grinned. 'All right. Be quick.'

He was about to go but turned back and
kissed my hand gallantly, signalling that a certain
formality had returned to his treatment of me
now I was no longer a schoolboy.

'It's been a privilege to share rooms with Tom
Cat. Don't disappear so entirely that we don't
know where you are, will you?'

'Of course not. Now off you go!' I pushed
him out the door.

Standing by the window, I watched Frank
moving from boy to boy in the Dean's Yard. It
was like watching a ripple pass across a pool as
the message spread. Then, so quickly it was hard
to see what started it, a scuffle broke out in one
corner. Richmond was going hammer and tongs

with Frank's friend, Mouthy Southey. The fight spread like wildfire as planter boys leapt to Richmond's defence, only to find themselves beset by the pro-abolition boys. I was pleased to see that Richmond was getting a good pasting and Fatty Ingels was buried under several burly bodies. Dr Vincent then strode out of his rooms, swishing his cane at anyone in reach, and shouting for order. Time for me to go.

I crept down the stairs and out into the quad. The noise of stamping, yelling and punching was impressive – not unlike one of Syd's boxing matches. Keeping close to the wall, I walked swiftly towards the lodge, carrying the coal scuttle to hide my bundle. I thought I had almost made it to safety when I came face to face with the Prince of Wales, Mr Sheridan and Mr Castleton proceeding at the double towards the disturbance.

'A scrap, eh what?' chuckled the Prince. 'Excellent – like to see a bit of boyish high spirits. Makes men of them, doesn't it, Sherry?'

Mr Sheridan recognized me instantly; Mr

Castleton looked as though he was trying to place me. My patron came to my rescue.

'Very true, your highness. Mr Castleton, is that not a most venerable oak over there? How old is it, would you say?' He pointed to the other side of the yard with his cane. 'I bet it's seen more than its fair share of battles.'

Mr Castleton tore his gaze from me to reply. The prince had never even noticed the maid in his path. I bobbed a curtsey but the heir to the throne marched straight by, heading for the oak.

Fortunately, the porter had left his post to help restore order in the yard. I slipped out through the postern and trotted as fast as I could in my clumsy shoes towards Westminster Bridge. It was only when I had crossed the Thames and was heading south-west across the scrubby fields of Lambeth that I felt able to breathe freely. I had done it: I'd escaped and no one at Westminster School would ever know what happened to Thomas Bennington-Smythe. I'd probably become a school legend as the boy who tricked his way to free food and lodging for several weeks, but my true identity would remain a secret.

The days are very short at this time of year so it was already dusk as I made my escape. Highwaymen are still occasionally to be met with on the roads out of London, particularly in the wilder parts such as the tenter grounds of Lambeth where only laundresses, tanners and huntsmen choose to come. I wouldn't be able to reach my destination safely on foot at night and I did not have the funds to travel by carriage. My best bet was to find shelter and continue at first light.

A chilly wind blew over the empty flats along the riverbank. A bird called forlornly from a thicket. Ice crunched underfoot as my clogs sunk through the surface into a foul-smelling rut full of water. Clutching my bundle to me for comfort, I had the weirdest sensation of being watched, but each time I turned, I saw no one on the deserted path I'd taken. My instincts told me to get out of sight quickly.

Finding an abandoned wash house, I let myself in. From the scuffling in a corner, I guessed that other creatures had sought this shelter from the cold, but I did not begrudge them as long as they did not disturb me. I was more concerned that other humans might take refuge here. I sat with my back to the old stove and shivered, wishing it would light again to give me some warmth. As the temperatures dropped, I thought longingly of my warm berth in the Sparrow's Nest and wished I had thought to steal a blanket from Frank.

I woke up in the middle of the night with a start as something cracked like a pistol shot.

'Donna fret, lassie,' said a husky voice. 'I just makin' up the fire.'

Light flickered on the ceiling from a small blaze in the centre of the wash house floor, smoke finding its way out through the numerous slipped tiles above. Crouched over it was a wrinkled old woman with one tooth and a pair of bright eyes. She had a tattered shawl over her head and straw wrapped around her feet for warmth. I felt for my bundle, but it lay exactly where I'd left it.

'Nae one's robbed you,' she laughed, 'though they might've if I hadna been here. Twae laddies came by, but I told them to gae away.'

I felt a little ashamed that I'd suspected her so quickly. 'Thank you. I'm really grateful. It's all I've got.'

'Aye,' the old woman said, 'I thought as much. You mun be down on your luck if you end up in auld Jean's washhouse.'

'This is yours?'

She nodded. 'The best laundry in London until I could nae lift the water and heat the stove. Auld age is a cruel thing when a body's no bairns to look after them.

'In that case, I'm sorry that I'm trespassing, but I was cold and it was getting late.'

'It's no sin to come here, lassie. If you give me one of them coppers of yours, I'll even let you come nigh the fire.'

So she had checked what was in my bundle then.

'Thank you, mother, that's very kind of you.' I felt in my bundle and drew out the purse. It was a shilling short.

'I took a wee coin for the night's lodging,' Old Jean chuckled.

A shilling was a lot of money for a hard floor and a patchy roof over my head, but I was in no position to argue.

'I'll stay where I am,' I said with regret. 'I really can't afford any more.'

'Suit yourself, lassie,' she said with a disappointed frown. 'You get some sleep now. I'll make sure nae one disturbs you – that's worth a shilling at least.'

The remainder of the night passed uneasily. I had no doubt that Old Jean saw me as a welcome source of income. She had designs on the rest of the purse, but I could not let her strip me of every penny as my own future was as uncertain as hers. I slept curled round my bundle, and was mighty relieved to see the dawn.

'Breakfast, my chick?' Old Jean asked as I rose, offering me an oatcake.

I shook my head – that was bound to be a penny at least. 'Thank you for your hospitality, mother. I wish you good day.'

'A fine-spoken lassie like you mun be able to spare me another shilling,' she begged, struggling to her feet and holding out a scrawny hand. 'I dare say a lassie like you has a few guineas at least sewn into her bodice.'

If only.

'I swear I don't, mother.' Holding the bundle in front of me to protect myself from her groping fingers, I moved rapidly to the door, sensing that her mood was changing. She gave a shrill whistle. Two rough-looking lads bounded into the hut through a hole in the back wall like a pair of eager hounds.

'At her, my lads!' Old Jean croaked. 'I'll wager me tooth that she's got more about her than in that wee pursie.'

I was out the front like a rabbit bolting from a hole. Hitching up my skirts, I ran towards the road. The clumsy clogs hampered me. One came off in a rut, the other I abandoned. Unlike my pursuers, I had the advantage of a few weeks of good food courtesy of Westminster School. I sprinted as fast as any boy and spotted a cart. It was driven by a milkman, returning from his deliveries in the city. Vaulting the fence, I jumped up beside the startled dairyman.

'Please protect me!' I gasped. 'They're trying to rob me.'

The man turned in his seat and saw the two skinny boys scrambling over the fence. He flicked his long whip at them.

'Be off with you, you rascals,' he said. 'And tell Old Jean that if she sends you after any more girls, I'll send the beadle after her.'

Like dogs called off by their master, the boys wheeled around and bounded back the way they had come, all the while yelling obscenities over their shoulder.

'And you, young miss, should learn not to mix with the likes of Old Jean,' he said with a shake of his head. 'Don't go accepting shelter from anyone you don't know.'

'I didn't, sir. I found her place empty and needed somewhere to sleep the night,' I said, still panting, 'but thank you.'

'That's all right, miss. Now, where you be going so early?'

'To Clapham.'

He dug into his apron and pulled out an apple. 'Well, you stay where you are and break your fast with me. I'm going that way and it'll save those bare feet of yours to sit up here.'

'How much will it cost, sir?' I asked tentatively. 'You see I don't have much money.'

'Nothing.' I must have looked surprised for he laughed. 'It was a rare treat to see you outrun Old Jean's beagles and leap the fence like a champion in a steeplechase – that's payment enough for Elias Jones. Now where did a girl like you learn to do that, eh? That's what I want to know.'

'You wouldn't believe me if I told you,' I replied with a shake of my head. I took the apple. 'Thank you, Mr Jones, I gladly accept your offer.'

Mr Jones dropped me at the edge of Clapham Common and I headed into the village. Clapham was a strange place these days, its rural centre surrounded by the stylish villas of rich incomers who were building all around the edge of the Common. Now farmers mixed with sea captains and members of parliament. I wasn't sure exactly where I was going, but I knew how I would tell if I had found the right place. I walked past the church – a lively matins was in progress with bells ringing – no good. I went up to the door of a chapel and found the Methodists singing hymns with gusto. That wasn't it. Finally I found what I was looking for: a small, simple building set back from the road. It was completely silent – only the open door indicated that the worshippers were present for their early morning meeting. I slipped in at the back and took a moment for my eyes to adjust to the gloom. There were only a few people present so I moved to an empty chair in the circle and waited.

The hush was so complete that I began to notice even the smallest movements. For example, I knew the exact moment that Miss Miller senior noticed my presence from the sharp intake of breath. Miss Prudence gave away her consternation by the clasping and unclasping of her hands. In a flutter, Miss Fortitude dropped her handkerchief. I knew what they were thinking: Drury Lane had invaded the Quaker Meeting House and they were desperate that no one else should notice.

An elderly man stood up. 'I feel moved by the Spirit to speak,' he said in a sonorous voice. 'I sense that some of my sisters are oppressed in spirit and need to be reminded to cast their cares on the Lord.'

'Amen,' intoned all present, except me. I was intending to cast my cares on the Miss Millers.

The meeting relapsed into silence. To be honest with you, Reader, it was torture for me. I am not in the habit of sitting five seconds in company without speaking, let alone half an hour. My mind was racing with so many things – my anxiety for Pedro, my fear that the Miss Millers would turn me away, my narrow escape from Old Jean. I couldn't wait for the meeting to end. The minutes crawled by. To this day, I still do not know what signalled the end of the worship, but suddenly everyone was on their feet, greeting each other with good wishes for the morning ahead. As a stranger, I was surrounded by people warmly welcoming me to the congregation. Only the Miss Millers did not approach. They were standing in a huddle, conferring as to what they should do. I decided to grab the bull by the horns.

'Miss Miller,' I said loudly, curtseying to the sisters, 'I'm so pleased to see you again.'

'Child, dost thou know our dear sisters in Christ?' asked the elderly man who had spoken in the meeting.

'Indeed, I do, Mr –?'

'Brother Andrew, child.'

'I came all this way to see them, Brother Andrew,' I confided.

Miss Miller senior, seeing me talking to one of the meeting house elders, bustled over.

'Sister Patience, dost thou know this child?' he asked, laying a fatherly hand on my shoulders. He glanced down at my bare, muddy feet. 'She seems in some need.'

'Indeed, I do, Brother Andrew. My sisters and I were just going to invite her to our house to refresh herself. Wilt thou come, Sister Catherine?'

'Thank you.' I felt a great sense of relief – my guess that the Miss Millers would not fail to help someone in distress had been right.

'Ah, then thou shalt be blessed,' Brother Andrew declared, raising his eyes to heaven, 'for some of us have entertained angels unawares, thou knows it well.'

'I'm sorry but I'm not an angel,' I said quickly, not wanting him to get the wrong impression. I was probably the least angelic girl he'd ever meet.

'Angels come in all guises, Sister Catherine,' he said with a smile that felt like summer sunshine on that cold day. 'Go with the sisters and take your rest.'

SCENE 3 – SILENCE IS GOLDEN

I followed the Miss Millers outside and trailed after them as they made their way back to their cottage. This was a pretty, rustic building with a thatched roof, whitewashed walls and lattice windows. A hedge of holly arched over the gate, looking very festive with its bright berries. Miss Miller opened the front door and waited as we all filed past her. She looked around to check no neighbours were watching, shut the door and turned to me, hands on her hips.

'Well, this is a surprise. May I enquire what thou dost here?'

I laced my hands together, scrutinizing each sister in turn. Miss Miller was the most formidable – her expression alert, her movements vigorous. Miss Prudence was the most excitable: her eyes bright. Miss Fortitude was the most timorous – she looked plain scared. All of them looked honest – all of them trustworthy. This was essential for I was going to have to put my faith in them if I was going to tell them the truth.

'I've been having a rather extraordinary few weeks since we last met,' I confessed. 'May I sit down and I'll tell you what's happened? All I ask is, at the end, you tell me if I can stay for a while.'

I took a deep breath and plunged into my tale.

'In all my life, I've never heard anything like it!' said Miss Miller when I'd finished.

'You theatre types certainly lead interesting lives,' said Miss Prudence, hugging herself with excitement. 'I wish I'd seen you punch that bully!'

'Prudence!' rapped out Miss Miller severely. 'Remember, we never approve of violence.'

Miss Fortitude got up without a word and filled the kettle.

'What dost thou, sister?' asked Miss Miller.

'I'm preparing a bath for our guest,' she replied meekly.

'But we haven't yet decided if she is to stay!' protested her elder.

Miss Fortitude drew herself up to her full five feet and faced her sister. 'Of course she stays. Our life is dedicated to helping those in distress. She has suffered because of the persecution of wicked men. Thou durst not turn her away.'

Miss Miller and Miss Prudence both looked shocked to hear their timid sister rebel, but then the elder regained her composure.

'Sister Catherine, look what thou hast done! Thou hast been under our roof but an instant and already Drury Lane begins to work on my sisters.' My stomach clenched in a knot of panic: was Miss Miller about to throw me out? Then her stern face relaxed into a smile as she turned to her youngest sister. 'But well said, Fortitude. I have always thought thou art too compliant – thou dost what is right. But let us first use the water for tea, then a bath. Our sister has passed a comfortless night and is in more need of breakfast than cleanliness.'

'But what will we tell our brothers and sisters?' asked Miss Prudence. 'Her connection to the theatre will be most difficult for us to explain.'

'Then we say nothing on the subject. Indeed, my conscience is clear on this point for we are duty bound to keep silent. Sister Catherine's origins must not be broadcast to the whole congregation – that would put her at risk,' said Miss Miller.

Her sisters were very relieved by this comfortable doctrine.

'You mean, silence is golden?' I asked archly.

'That's precisely what I mean,' smiled Miss Miller.

This pronouncement opened the gates on a flood of kindness from the sisters. Under their gentle ministrations, I was fed, washed and clothed. It was a particular relief to have a proper bath in front of the kitchen fire as I'd not had one for many months.

'No shoes!' tutted Miss Prudence as she tied one of her aprons over the too-big dress I had been given. They were all small women, but even so their clothes swamped me.

'I'll go to Mrs Jones. She has a brood of children: we should be able to borrow some clothes the right size for Sister Catherine,' said Miss Miller, putting on her bonnet. 'I will get some milk while I'm there. Young people need more milk than us oldsters.'

Miss Miller sallied out with Miss Fortitude, leaving me alone with Miss Prudence. She took a comb and began to tackle my hair.

'I always wanted long red hair like you had,' she confided in me. Her own white locks peeped out from under her cap – she really was very pretty with her heart-shaped face and periwinkle blue eyes. She must have been stunning as a girl. 'It shows that thou dost not suffer from the sin of vanity when thou sacrificed thy hair to a greater cause.'

'Oh, I'm vain enough,' I confessed, 'but I don't think I've much to be vain about. Now, Lizzie, Lady Elizabeth, that's who I think of as being beautiful.'

Miss Prudence smiled and tucked my hair behind my ears.

'Promise you won't tell?' she asked me conspiratorially.

'Of course,' I replied, wondering what secret she was about to reveal.

She moved to her workbag and pulled out a length of green ribbon. 'I can't resist pretty things. I have lots and lots of them hidden away.'

'Why don't you wear them in your cap? You'd look lovely.'

She fastened the ribbon in my hair. 'We don't approve of such vanities. We like things to be plain, simple and serviceable.'

'But the world won't come to an end if you wear just a little one,' I coaxed her. 'Please show me your collection. I can't be the only one wearing ribbons.'

With great pride, Miss Prudence laid out her rainbow of silks and satins. I picked out a blue one and tied it around her white cap.

'There! That matches your eyes.'

Miss Prudence giggled and patted her head nervously. 'I feel very wicked,' she admitted.

'I'm sure God likes you to feel that sort of wicked as it doesn't harm anyone.'

This idea delighted her. 'Sister Catherine, I think thou art in the right. One ribbon will not bring the meeting house down about our ears.'

Miss Prudence and I spent a happy hour chatting about the theatre until her two sisters returned in triumph. They bore a can of milk and a pair of shoes only one size too big.

'Mrs Jones had heard of thy escape already,' said Miss Miller, pouring me a large glass of milk. Her eyes slid to her sister's cap but she made no comment. 'Her husband carried thee here.'

'Elias! He was very kind,' I said, taking a sip. The milk tasted so fresh and creamy, unlike the thin stuff I had in town, which was watered down and mixed with flour. 'Is he a Quaker too?'

Miss Prudence laughed. 'No, he is one of those Methodistical fellows – fine folk, if a little too noisy for our taste. And fie, Sister Catherine, if thou stayest among us, thou must not call us Quakers. We are the Society of Friends.'

I blushed. 'I'm sorry, I was told you were called Quakers.'

'That's what some call us,' nodded Miss Miller, picking up her knitting and making herself comfortable in her chair, 'because, when the Spirit moves, we have been known to quiver and shake in the presence of our Maker. But it also can be taken to mean our desire to rock the foundations of injustice and bring the house of slavery crashing to the ground. We work to make God's kingdom come on earth and slavery has no part in that heavenly society where all shall be friends.'

This sounded all very well, but, in my opinion, there was a flaw in her view of the world.

'I don't think I can be friends with men like Kingston Hawkins,' I said.

'Even him, Sister Catherine. He also is a child of his Maker though he has left the path of truth. One day the lion shall lie with the lamb. Thou must pray for him.'

This seemed a very tall order. 'I'm not sure I can,' I replied. 'I think he's still at the stage where he'll eat the lamb if he so much as catches a glimpse of a shake of its tail.'

Miss Miller smiled and let the matter drop.

Time passed slowly as I waited to hear news of Pedro. It was difficult to contain my impatience but I knew that I could be of no help until we had a sign that he was being moved to the port. In the meanwhile, I was faced with a new challenge: behaving myself. I had never lived in such a sober, industrious household with regular mealtimes, prayers and early to bed. No one had ever expected me to act like a polite young lady before. I found it quite a struggle to fit in, not least since I had been playing a boy for the past few weeks.

'Sister Catherine, a lady does not sit with her knees apart in that rude fashion,' rapped out Miss Miller as I lolled in a chair during the evening Bible reading.

I sat up straight and put my hands in my lap. I really didn't want to offend my kind hosts. Boredom took over again and I began twiddling my thumbs absent-mindedly. A basket of sewing was dumped in my lap.

'The Devil makes work for idle hands,' said Miss Fortitude sweetly.

Whistling, running, jumping, laughing too boisterously – all were out. I had to school myself to sit quietly, keep my back straight and my deportment correct. Miss Miller also said I was to keep my thoughts godly, but she agreed that this might be a step beyond my capabilities for the present.

I had started by liking the Miss Millers for their kindness, but as the days passed, I grew to admire them too. I had imagined that they were quiet, retiring sorts, but I was proved wrong. They were running an empire every bit as big as Billy Shepherd's, though with a far different purpose. Miss Miller corresponded with Quakers in every corner of the country and even abroad as she spread the word about the abolition movement. The cottage was a hive of political activity. The post boy came to the gate every day bearing letters. He and I were soon on first name terms. From what he told me, I was surprised the Miss Millers had any money left, for so much went paying the carrier's charges.

Their lives had so much more purpose than my own shiftless existence. If only they would allow themselves a little more fun . . .

Act V - In which Kingston
Hawkins is taught the meaning
of brotherhood...

ACT V

SCENE 1 – CARGO ON THE MOVE

Snow was falling thick and fast as four demure Quaker women descended from a hackney carriage and mounted the steps to a very fine house in Grosvenor Square, whose windows blazed with candlelight. The door opened immediately.

Word had reached Mr Equiano that Hawkins showed signs of leaving England; none of us doubted that he'd try to take Pedro with him. Having decided that I was unlikely to be spotted among so many visitors, it had been agreed that I could risk attending the meeting that night. To be doubly sure, only Joseph was on duty as the most trustworthy of all the staff.

'Ladies, if you will follow me to the library,' he said without even pausing to take our street clothes.

As we entered the book-filled room, I saw

at once that there were no children playing on the ladders today. My heart ached for the boy who'd taken the trip with me along the shelves. But, though there were some here who might have been game on another occasion, at this emergency meeting of the abolitionists, we all felt far too serious to indulge in horseplay.

The duchess moved between her guests, greeting rich and poor alike with her inimitable brand of good humour. Among the other abolitionists already gathered, I recognized Elias Jones.

'Pleased to see you in better company, Miss Fence-Jumper,' he said after bowing to the sisters.

'Very much better, thanks to you.' I looked around the gathering – all sections of society were present from peers to paupers, the latter represented in my own person. 'Talking of company, our cause seems to have quite a levelling effect, wouldn't you say, Mr Jones?'

'Aye, miss, that it does,' he agreed, following

my thought. 'We don't need a revolution like them Frenchies to bring us together in fellowship. But still, I found it very strange coming to the front door, being used to delivering round the back of houses like this.'

I liked him for his honesty. 'Me too. It was only Pedro who had the nerve to ring the front door bell when we came for the first time.'

'Poor lad,' murmured Mr Jones. 'I hope we can save him but I fear we'd better pray for a miracle.'

'Amen,' said Miss Miller.

Seeing us standing in a corner, the duchess sallied over.

'I've come to thank you for taking in our little stray,' she addressed the sisters. 'You're perfect saints, all three of you.'

'They have to be to put up with me,' I said, receiving her hearty kiss on both cheeks.

Lizzie followed her mother, bringing with her someone I didn't want to see again.

'Cat, I don't think you've met my very dear

friend Milly Hengrave, have you?' said Lizzie mischievously.

I blushed and curtsied clumsily to Charlie's sister. 'Pleased to make your acquaintance, Miss Hengrave.'

Milly looked straight at me. 'Good gracious! Do you know you bear a stunning resemblance to my brother's old room mate? You don't have a twin by any chance?'

I coughed. 'Er, no, Miss Hengrave.'

There was an awkward pause, then Milly, Lizzie and the duchess all burst into laughter.

'I know all about it,' said Milly, wiping her eyes. 'Little brother, I'm delighted to meet you. I've heard so much about you from Charlie. My, how you've . . . shrunk since I last saw you in Ireland.'

I relaxed and returned her friendly smile. 'The real Thomas is going to have trouble when he gets to school if he's as big as Charlie says. The Latin teacher has him earmarked for all the female roles in classical drama.'

'And how are you, Cat?' Lizzie asked. 'Frank and I were so worried until we received your note.'

'I'm fine. Only scared for Pedro.'

Lizzie's smile faded. 'I know. Syd's been keeping an eye on the river. He's got boys posted on all the landing places. When Hawkins does make his move, the key will be to act swiftly to get the *habeas corpus* from a magistrate.'

'Where is Syd? Is he coming?'

'He's sorry he can't be here, Cat. He's got a match. He's sending one of his boys along.'

The abolitionists began to take their places in the circle of chairs prepared for them. As the crowd thinned, Charlie and Frank came over to greet me.

'Miss Bennington-Smythe, a pleasure as always,' said Frank, bending over my hand a little stiffly.

'How are the scars?' I asked.

'A trifle compared to what your persecutors got. I am pleased to report that the planters were soundly beaten.'

'The Prince of Wales was most displeased,' chipped in Charlie.

'Oh? I thought he rather relished the sport.'

'He did. But when he found out what it was about, he placed a wager on the planters with Mr Sheridan.'

Mr Equiano appeared at my shoulder and placed a welcoming hand on my arm. 'His Royal Highness favours the pro-slavery cause, you know, like the rest of the royal family,' he said levelly.

'I didn't.' That was depressing news. If the king himself was against abolition, it was hard to imagine the cause making much progress in parliament.

'I'm pleased to see you in a safe harbour, Miss Royal,' Mr Equiano continued, nodding at the Miss Millers. 'Let us hope we can soon say the same thing about our boy.'

As the meeting got under way, I looked round the room for Syd's representative, but I could not see anyone I recognized. My curiosity was satisfied when I heard a commotion outside. Joseph strode into the room closely followed by Nick, both looking very excited.

'We have news at last, your grace!' Joseph announced to the duchess, quite forgetting his station as he burst in upon the meeting.

Nick bent double to regain his breath. 'Just found out. They've moved the cargo. Pedro was put on board this evenin'. '

'Which ship? Where?' asked Mr Sharp, alert for action.

'The *Jenny Wren*, Captain Taylor. It's lying in the Pool on the Greenwich side of the river.'

'Right, let's go!' said Mr Sharp to Mr Equiano. 'We'll tackle Sir John Solmes and get the writ. Gentlemen, we'll leave you to hold the ship until we arrive.'

In the general bustle to leave, Nick wormed his way over to me and shook my hand. 'Good to see you again, Cat.'

'And you, Nick. Whom do we have to thank for tonight's news?'

Nick shrugged. 'Don't know 'is name – a little ragged fellow, though 'e ponged of fish sure enough. You know, Cat, I think Shepherd is tryin' to be clever. 'E thought Syd'd be too busy to notice but the Billingsgate lads were on to 'is game. I've got to go and tell Syd now. You stay put. I'll see you back 'ere – with the Prince, I 'ope.'

Nick darted out the way he had come. Soon after, Frank and Charlie left with Mr Sharp and Mr Equiano. Elias Jones, a determined look on his face, led the remaining men off to find the *Jenny Wren* and keep her in port. Soon only we women remained behind, sitting around the fire in silence.

'What do we do now?' I asked, wishing I had some task I could perform. I hated having to wait for others to act.

'Let us pray for our brothers, particularly Brother Pedro,' said Miss Miller, folding her hands and closing her eyes.

And all of us did pray, or tried to. Heavenly guidance or my own restlessness, I've no idea, but my thoughts kept returning to the boy who'd brought the message – the boy Nick did not know. It was like an itch I couldn't quite reach to scratch. You see, I'd been caught out by Billy Shepherd that way before. He'd once used a stranger to lure me into the Rookeries. Nick had said Shepherd was clever, but I knew him to be more than that: he was the most devious person alive. If his name was wrapped up in a bit of business, I'd bet my last farthing that it was not what it seemed, that he would have twisted it in some way to his advantage. Look at his invitation to see Pedro: he'd wanted to take me so he could control what we did with the information. He loved to be in charge. Putting myself in his smelly shoes for a moment, he would have guessed that Syd was having him watched. He knew we were waiting for him to move Pedro to the river. Would he really carry Pedro on board without trying to distract us from his purpose? It was too straightforward – therefore, it wasn't right.

'It's a diversion,' I announced suddenly to the silent room.

'What's that you say, child?' asked Miss Miller, her eyes snapping open.

'Billy Shepherd – he's sending us on a wild goose chase. The messenger boy was a decoy. If he's sent a message that Pedro's on the south side of the river, you can bet that he's on the north.' I was on my feet, tying on my bonnet.

'That's preposterous!' exclaimed Miss Miller.

'Are you sure?' said the duchess, frowning.

'Yes, positive. I know Billy Shepherd better than most, possibly better than anyone. I know what he's doing.'

'Where are you going, Cat?' asked Lizzie. I had my hand on the doorknob.

I couldn't understand why they were all staring at me. Didn't they realize that we had a job to do? 'Well, I for one can't just sit here. We've got to chase the men and tell them they're going the wrong way. And some of us have to find the right ship. Come on.'

Lizzie was the first to get over her surprise and place her confidence in my instincts. She got up. 'You're right. Mama, you and I must go after Mr Sharp. Where should we bring them?'

'Try Billingsgate – that's where I'm starting.'

'That you most certainly are not!' protested Miss Miller. 'We can't let you wander around the docks at this time of night on your own.'

'Then we'd better not let her go on her own, sister,' said Miss Fortitude resolutely, buttoning up her gloves.

'I'll send for a cab,' said Miss Prudence, disappearing out of the door.

'And someone had better fetch Syd. Where was his match, Lizzie?'

'In a tavern on Fleet Street.'

We looked at each other. A woman going in a place like that on her own would have to have a lot of guts, particularly if she was about to stop a match in its tracks.

'I'll go,' volunteered Milly, picking up her umbrella. 'Can you lend me a footman or two?'

The duchess nodded. 'Of course. Joseph and one of the others will accompany you. No, hang that! There must be ten of those lazy doorstops around the place – take them all. It's about time they earned their keep. We'll rendezvous in Billingsgate.'

Mrs Jones, the farmer's wife to whom I owed my shoes, offered to go in pursuit of her husband. That settled, we parted in the lobby as the hackney cabs and carriages drew up.

'Cat, good luck!' called Milly as she waved me off in the cab. Lizzie was too late to hush her. Well, if anyone heard, I could do nothing about it. I had no time to worry about my own safety. Our efforts would count for nothing if we could not find Pedro's ship before it sailed on the tide. Once he left British waters, no magistrate's writ would save him.

I could tell we were arriving in Billingsgate by the smell. The market lay quiet this time of night – the fishwives would only return to gut the catch and screech at each other when the boats came in early in the morning. The reek of fish forced itself into our lungs. Miss Fortitude put her handkerchief to her nose; the rest of us sat stoically, trying not to take deep breaths.

The cab could go no further. The jarvey pulled the horse to a standstill. The wharves were dark. Stacks of boxes stood on the quayside, creating a confusing labyrinth of passageways. I wondered how I was going to find the Billingsgate gang in all of this.

'What are you going to do, Sister Catherine?' asked Miss Miller, for the first time looking to me for leadership. She must have been feeling very out of her depth to relinquish command; to tell the truth, I felt pretty much in over my head too.

'There must be someone around – a night watchman at least,' I said with more confidence than I felt. I knew from watching Mr Kemble that even when you realized you were appearing in a play destined to be a flop, you had to soldier on as if it were the greatest show on earth in order to bring the rest of the cast with you. 'We should get out and look. Tell the jarvey to wait here for us – we might need to make a fast retreat if we run into trouble.'

Standing on the cold pavement while Miss Miller passed on this instruction I looked about, trying to find some clue to help me. The crates all bore ice toppings an inch deep. The passageways were under drifts of untouched snow. All except one. The snow had been beaten flat by the passage of boots – some people had passed this way recently. That was enough for me.

'Follow me,' I told my companions.

With only the swish of our skirts to give away our presence, we trod lightly down the path between the stacks of crates. The trail led us on to the quayside. A rim of ice like broken glass had formed on the water's edge. The Thames spread out before us, inky black except where the surface reflected the glitter of lights from the many vessels at anchor. Somewhere in the distance, laughter and music floated out of the open door of a tavern. From a nearby ship, a piper played a sad, strange melody, accompanied by the soft heartbeat of a drum. At the far end of the quay, a brazier burned, the shadow of a man flickered beside it.

'That might be the watchman,' I said without too much hope. I didn't like this place – it should be full of people and life, not dark and creepy as it was now.

'We're with thee, Cat,' said Miss Prudence.

'And the Lord is with us,' added Miss Miller.

With this encouragement, I set off towards the man warming his hands by the brazier.

When we were within earshot, I called out, 'Excuse me, sir, can you spare me a moment?'

He turned slowly, tipping his hat on to the back of his head, and grinned.

'Course I can, Cat. I've been waitin' for you.'

Billy Shepherd – of course.

'Who's this young man, Sister Catherine?' asked Miss Miller. 'Is he a friend of thine?'

I was momentarily lost for words. My mind

was in a whirl as I tried to work out what his presence here meant.

'Well, lady,' said Shepherd in an unusually polite tone for him, 'you could say that. Cat and I go back a long way. We know each other well. She knew what I'd done, and I knew what she'd do. No way would she tumble for the boy trick twice. And it's worked out far better than even I 'oped with 'er turnin' up before the bone'ead boxer and 'is 'eavy mob.'

'Boy trick? What hast thou done?' Miss Miller was understandably confused. 'Art thou one of the Billingsgate boys we are looking for?'

Time to disabuse my companions. 'No, Miss Miller, he's not. He's Billy Shepherd, Pedro's gaoler,' I explained, glaring at him.

'Aw, Cat, I wouldn't put it like that. I provided Blackie with temporary accommodation of the 'ighest standard for a small remuneration.' He dug into the brazier with a shovel and poured something out on to his gloved hand. 'Chestnut anyone?'

'You know where you can shove that chestnut, Boil,' I hissed, feeling a familiar surge of anger. He was loving this – every minute of my bewilderment.

'Sister Catherine!' exclaimed Miss Miller.

'Don't fret, lady,' laughed Shepherd. 'I'm used to her tongue. She only says these things 'cos she likes me so much.'

I ignored them both. 'Just tell me where Pedro is.'

'No.' He cracked the chestnut shell in his fist and popped the sweet white nut into his mouth, watching me all the while.

'Tell me!' I yelled at him, stamping my foot. Every minute he wasted could mean that Pedro's ship had time to set sail. 'Tell me or I'll –'

'Or you'll do what, Cat?' grinned Billy. 'Sure you don't want a nut? They're very good. Nicked them meself on me way 'ere – just for old times' sake, to keep me 'and in.'

I couldn't think what I'd do, except perhaps self-destruct in an explosion of pure temper.

Fortunately, my companions were not so clueless.

'Or she'll pray for you,' said Miss Miller, stepping in front of me. 'Come on, sisters, let us lay our hands on our errant brother and bring him to the Lord.' The three Miss Millers swooped on Billy before he had time to react and hooked him with their tiny fists.

'Oi! Get off!' protested Billy. It wasn't his style to lower himself to beat off three elderly ladies. Besides, the Miss Millers' grip was surprisingly tenacious after all those years of needle-work and letter-writing.

'Oh, Father, lookest Thou on this miserable sinner, William Shepherd. Change his heart, Oh Lord. Make him obedient to Your Will,' intoned Miss Miller.

'Amen,' replied her sisters.

'Cleanse him with hyssop so that he may repent and lead a new life to Thy Glory,' trilled Miss Prudence.

'Amen,' went the response.

'Cat, call 'em off,' said Billy. He looked

worried. Perhaps the Miss Millers had tapped into a hitherto unsuspected strain of religious belief in Shepherd? The sight gave me great pleasure.

I gave him an angelic smile and closed my eyes, placing my hand on his sleeve. 'Though his soul is now as ugly as his outer person, create in him a new heart so that he may lead us in the right way,' I prayed.

'Nah, Cat, not you. You're not allowed to get religion!' he protested, trying to prise my fingers from his jacket.

'Yea, even though he is but a worm in Thy sight, Thou carest for the unrighteous as much as the righteous,' said Miss Fortitude, getting into the swing of our impromptu prayer meeting.

But my kind friends were not to know that Shepherd had a temper to match mine or perhaps they would not have drawn so close to him. It now boiled over.

'Get off me, you old witches!' he shouted, shaking himself free.

'Oh Lord . . .!' began Miss Miller, about to

take hold again but I saw it just in time. Billy flicked his wrist. A knife appeared in his hand. I pulled Miss Miller back by the skirt. His swipe missed us both.

'He tried to knife Patience!' exclaimed Miss Fortitude in a shocked voice.

'Of course he did,' I said bitterly. 'He's Billy Shepherd, not the Good Shepherd. Look, Billy, leave my friends alone. You've got no quarrel with them.'

Shepherd smoothed down his rumpled jacket, annoyed that he had lost his composure in front of us. 'You're right, Cat. When I 'eard from Old Jean they'd taken you in, I knew they must be daft cows. Now I've seen it for meself.'

'You knew where I was?'

'Course, Moggy. Someone 'as to keep an eye on you. You're too dangerous to let out of sight for long.'

The reach of his influence unnerved me. He was a formidable person to have as an enemy.

'I could say the same about you,' I conceded.

'And you'd be right. Sounds to me as if we're made for each other.' He gave me a strange smile.

'Made to torment each other, you mean.'

He just shrugged at that.

Miss Miller had now recovered from almost being skewered by one of the London under-world's most infamous characters. 'Sister Catherine, can this man help us or not? We have no time to waste,' she asked sharply, casting a less than charitable look at her assailant.

I gazed straight at him, wondering the same thing. 'Why were you waiting for me, Billy?'

He took another chestnut. 'That's better, Cat – back to business. You tell me why I'm here.'

'I can think of many reasons.'

'Go on.'

'To laugh at me as I lose my friend thanks to you?' He said nothing. 'Or perhaps you've a deal with Hawkins now and you plan to hand me over?' He spat a piece of shell into the brazier. 'Or maybe, now you've delivered your cargo, you're free to help me without ruining your reputation with the canting crew?'

He smiled. 'Now what makes you think I'd do that for you?'

He was right: why would he? 'Selfless' and 'Billy Shepherd' were three words that would never be used in the same sentence.

'There has to be something in it for you. You want something from . . . from me?'

'Very good, Cat. Now what would that be, do you think?'

He'd once wanted a diamond from me – but he knew I had no money now. I couldn't think of anything I had that he could possibly want.

'I don't know,' I admitted.

This answer pleased him immensely. 'I'm glad I'm not so predictable that even your mind-readin' powers are stumped. I'll tell you: I want you to be in me debt. I want you to leave 'ere tonight knowin' that you owe me somethink. Between you and me, Cat, there'll be an invisible chain which I can tug any time I want to call in my favour. 'Ow does that sound to you?'

It sounded terrifying. But did that matter? He was our only way to Pedro – so what if I had to bargain with the devil?

'All right – so long as –'

'No conditions, Moggy,' he interrupted.

How I hated his rotten grin! He had me – and he knew it.

'Sister Catherine, don't give your word. It's not wise,' whispered Miss Prudence.

'I know it's not – that's why he's doing it.' I crossed my fingers behind my back. 'All right, we have an agreement. Now, tell me where Pedro is.'

Shepherd's smile grew so broad, it looked as though he would crack his pimply face in two.

'I'll do better than that – I'll take you there meself.' He nodded down at the steps where a little vessel was tied up. 'You don't 'alf give value for money, Cat. Watchin' you work is an eddycation on its own. I wouldn't miss seein' you try and stop the captain and forty tars settin' sail when they want. Get in, ladies. We're bound for the *Phoenix*.'

I shook my head. 'Not all of us. Miss Fortitude and Miss Prudence, stay here and let the others know where we are. Your sister and I will do our best to delay the ship.'

'Aw, Cat, don't you think you're up to the job on your own?' he mocked.

Billy offered his hand to help Miss Miller into the boat, but I was pleased to see her refuse it with a sniff of disgust as she got in unaided. With her sisters watching us nervously from the quayside, we set off on to the river.

SCENE 2 – AM I NOT A MAN
AND A BROTHER?

Billy rowed us out to the *Phoenix*, whistling tunelessly between his teeth. The ship lay just downstream of London Bridge in the middle of the river. From the lights and activity on deck it looked suspiciously as if the captain was preparing to weigh anchor.

'Hurry, Billy,' I urged.

'Don't fret, Cat: they won't go just yet.'

His confidence was no comfort. As I watched the snowflakes settle and melt on his straining back, I wondered what other surprises he had in store for me. He had never said that he did not have another deal with Hawkins, and I would not put it past him to double-cross me.

Miss Miller sat at the other end of the boat, her head bowed. She only raised it as we neared the ship.

'Let me go first, Sister Catherine,' she said. 'The captain might listen to me if he is a godly man.'

Billy gave a snort of laughter and spat over the side. 'Captain Janssen, a godly man? Pah! You know wot, lady, you're almost as funny as Moggy 'ere.'

That did not sound very encouraging.

Billy put two fingers in his mouth and let out a sharp whistle. 'Ahoy there, *Phoenix*! Three to come aboard.'

A sailor peered over the side, holding out a lantern. Seeing there were ladies involved, he let down the chair – a piece of tackle a bit like a wooden swing – to hoist Miss Miller up. I did not wait for it to be lowered back down. I followed Billy up the rope ladder.

Arriving on deck, I saw Miss Miller in earnest conversation with a large man with white-blond hair, a hooked nose and a thin mouth – Captain Janssen. Billy lolled against the rail and waved me forward.

'At 'im, Cat! I won't get in the way if I watch from 'ere, will I?'

I gave him a sarcastic smile and hurried to Miss Miller's side. Twenty or so sailors had stopped work to watch the altercation.

'Thou art holding the boy against his will,' she was arguing. 'In the name of humanity, thou must let him free.'

'I am a reasonable man, lady,' rumbled the captain in a deep voice with a Scandinavian accent. 'But my passenger claims the boy is his servant. It is no business of mine to interfere.'

'But it is!' Miss Miller may have been almost a foot shorter in stature than the captain, but she made up for it in the grandeur of her manner. 'It is thy duty as a Christian to defend the weak.'

He seemed to find the idea highly amusing. 'Hey, you hear that, bosun – me, the defender of the weak!'

'Aye, captain, the weak don't last long on your ship. You give 'em a helping hand over the side if they're on the way out,' growled the bosun as he sucked on the stem of his pipe.

I shivered at these words. Of course Hawkins' preferred vessel would be owned by a slaver of the very worst sort – I should've anticipated that. We were not going to get anywhere by appealing to his better nature – he didn't have one.

'I have no time to talk religion with you, lady,' said Captain Janssen, turning away. 'I have a ship to take out on the tide and unless you want to come with me to Jamaica, I suggest you return to shore.'

Miss Miller hooked his arm with the end of her umbrella. 'I haven't finished with thee yet, my man,' she scolded. 'Don't they teach manners where thou comest from? Dost thou not know that it's rude to turn thy back to a lady?'

I guessed that Miss Miller also knew it was fruitless to try and win him over and had switched to doing her best to distract and delay him. If we could just make enough fuss to stop the ship sailing until Mr Sharp arrived, we might stand a chance of saving Pedro. I would use the time she had bought us to find my friend and see if I could set him free.

'Bosun, clear the deck of strangers,' Janssen growled.

'Not before I've taught thee how to behave as becomes a Christian gentleman,' cried Miss Miller in a shrill voice.

Entertained by Miss Miller's loud sermon to their captain as to the shortcomings in his upbringing, the crew did not try to stop me as I slipped away to search the ship. My hunt did not last long as no attempt had been made to hide Pedro. He was chained to the main mast, surrounded by a ring of gentlemen, chief among them Kingston Hawkins. My friend looked desperate, sitting with his arms around his legs, clearly freezing in the snowy weather.

'Your health, gentlemen,' Hawkins said, raising a glass to his companions. 'To my boy's happy homecoming.'

'You said Kemble would never get away with stealing him from you and you were right!' said an elderly man I recognized as Dr Juniper from the billiard room. 'You'll make an example of him when you get back, I suppose? This boy's a rotten apple – leave him in the barrel and the whole place will rot.'

'Oh yes, replied Hawkins, he'll hang high and hang long. There won't be any sad violins playing at his funeral.'

The gentleman laughed.

'Such a shame his capital value has been spoilt by all this. He could've made you a lot of money,' said another man, taking a pinch of snuff from a gold box.

'I'll willingly sacrifice all that to rub those abolitionists' noses in it when they see what they made me do to him.'

'You're a good man, Hawkins,' said Dr Juniper, patting him on the back.

They made me sick, these slavers! I could feel myself shaking with rage but now was no time for an outburst. I crept up silently to within feet of Pedro and hunkered down behind a coop of sleepy chickens, waiting for an opportunity to catch his attention. His eyes were closed and his lips moving soundlessly as if praying for a miracle. I wished I could reach out and touch him: he looked so alone.

While I was debating what best to do, I heard oars splashing in the darkness, followed by the bump of a vessel coming alongside. Next came raised voices from the stern.

'I say, what's going on?' asked Dr Juniper, looking up.

'Just some mad old woman trying to free that there slave of yours,' explained a passing sailor.

'Radicals and madmen,' said Dr Juniper, shaking his head. 'That's what the abolitionists are.'

'Tell Janssen to throw her over the side if he must. I want to set sail tonight,' ordered Hawkins.

But it wasn't just one old lady Janssen had to contend with: Mr Sharp and party had arrived, swarming up the rope ladder before anyone could stop them. Mr Sharp now appeared on the steps leading down to the main deck, waving a piece of paper, Frank, Charlie, Lizzie, the duchess, Miss Miller and Mr Equiano all behind him. Pedro lifted his head, hope in his eyes. Hawkins dropped his glass. It smashed on the deck, leaving a stain like blood on the planks.

'Mr Hawkins,' called out Mr Sharp. 'Mr Kingston Hawkins! I have here a writ against you for the immediate production of one Pedro Hawkins, late of Drury Lane. According to this, you have no right to remove the boy from England against his will.'

'Janssen!' roared Hawkins. 'Throw them off this ship!'

The captain stumped forward, his face pale with anger. 'I can't, sir. They'll never let me dock again if I ignore this. It'll ruin business. For God's sake, it's only one slave.'

'Only one slave!' bellowed Hawkins. 'This is about more than the boy – it's about what's mine and what isn't.'

'Exactly,' said Mr Equiano triumphantly,

'and the law says that Pedro isn't yours to take away against his will.'

Hawkins turned on the African. 'Shut your mouth, negro. I don't listen to the likes of you.'

'Well, you should,' said the duchess, sweeping across the deck towards him, impressive in her ermine-trimmed, salmon pink cape. 'Let the boy free or you'll be sorry.'

Hawkins gave her a humourless smile. 'Sorry to disappoint a lady and all that, but I know I'll be even sorrier if I let him go.'

'But you must, man,' reasoned Mr Sharp. 'Your captain can't sail with him on board.'

Hawkins bowed his head for a moment, thinking as he fiddled with the top of his cane.

'All right,' he said at last. 'All right, *habeas corpus*: you can have his corpse!' With a ringing sound, he pulled his sword from his stick and raised it to stab Pedro in the heart.

'No!' screamed Lizzie. A whole deck stretched between Mr Sharp's party and Pedro. I was the only one within reach. I grabbed the first thing that came to hand – a mop – and leapt from my hiding place, planting myself in front of Pedro to parry the blow. The stroke cut into the wood and stuck there, point towards my chest.

'Cat!' shouted Pedro. Lizzie screamed again.

'Not you!' hissed Hawkins. His blue eyes burned with hatred as he bore down on me. 'I'll kill you!' He pushed towards me, driving the blade closer. I was no match for his strength. But as the point pricked my throat, a flat disc flew out of the air from behind me and struck him on the forehead. He reeled, giving me time to execute Syd's emergency manoeuvre. Hawkins received a kick to his privates that brought tears to his eyes, the first he'd probably ever shed. That was enough – Frank and Charlie were on him, wrestling him to the floor. Mr Sharp and the duchess stood between Hawkins and the other gentlemen as they moved to his aid.

'You really don't want to cross the Duchess of Avon,' she said, raising her fan threateningly at

Dr Juniper. 'Or you'll be black-balled from every club in St James.'

Mr Equiano disarmed Hawkins, throwing the swordstick into the river. He then searched his pockets for the key to free Pedro from his chains.

'You'll regret this!' hissed Hawkins.

'I don't think so,' said Mr Equiano, unlocking Pedro's neck collar. 'We're free men – we're not afraid of you, Hawkins.' Mr Equiano then wrapped his cloak around Pedro and led him away from the mast, stepping on Hawkins in the process – doubtless by accident.

I meanwhile had retrieved the disc that had saved my life and took it back to its owner.

'A neat throw, Pedro,' I said, holding it out to him. 'I don't think Mr Wedgwood had thought of that usage when he made it, but it was certainly effective.'

'I just hope I've permanently stamped the message on his forehead,' Pedro replied with a shaky smile.

He reached out and took my hand fast in his,

our palms wrapped around the medallion. He then pulled me towards him and hugged me tight. I was in tears; from the heave of his shoulders, he was too.

But we weren't safe yet. We were still on board a slave ship that was about to set sail, heavily outnumbered by a hostile crew.

Frank and Charlie got off Hawkins and moved to join us. We formed a circle, Pedro in our midst.

'What now?' I asked Mr Equiano in a low voice. Hawkins had got up and hobbled over to rejoin his friends and Captain Janssen. They now entered into a hasty conference. It looked as though they were planning a counter-attack. Moments later, Janssen stepped forward.

'This is my ship. I cannot have you man-handling my passenger like that,' he declared.

'Of course, captain,' Mr Sharp said politely. 'But I cannot have him flouting the law. Now we have Pedro, we will disembark and leave you in peace.'

'No one's getting off. We're cleared to sail and I'm not going to miss this tide.' Janssen gave a nod and the sailors leapt up the rigging to unfurl the canvas.

Mr Sharp and Mr Equiano exchanged worried looks.

'Don't be ridiculous – put us ashore, man,' boomed the duchess.

'Of course, ma'am – as soon as is convenient. Gravesend, or maybe Portsmouth.'

I glanced fearfully at Pedro. I didn't fancy our chances of getting free if the *Phoenix* left the Thames.

'There's a boat approachin', captain,' called a sailor.

My hope rekindled. Surely by now it would be Syd's gang or Mr Jones and the men? Janssen must have thought the same thing.

'I've no time to take on more passengers. Weigh anchor!'

'Aye aye, captain.'

Then a whistle blew shrill in the night. 'Ahoy, *Phoenix*! Stop in the name of King

George,' came a voice from the waters below.

'It's the Bow Street runners,' shouted the bosun, peering out into the night. 'There's six of 'em packed like sardines in a lighter. We can't ignore 'em – they'll catch up with us down river if we do and there'll be hell to pay.'

A delighted smile spread across Hawkins' face. He looked across at me, sensing a consolation prize within his grasp. 'Yes, do stop, captain. I think they just want to relieve you of some unwanted cargo.'

I thought of making a run for it. Shepherd was still lounging against the rail, watching the drama unfold with a sardonic expression on his face. He might be prevailed upon to take me off before the runners had a chance to catch me. But Mr Equiano put a hand on my shoulder.

'Stay where you are,' he whispered as I made a move to bolt away. 'It will be all right.'

There was a pause as the runners climbed over the side. My old acquaintance, Constable Lennox, came first. He soon spotted me in the huddle around Pedro despite my much altered exterior.

'Captain, I've come to arrest that girl over there.' He pointed at me. 'And a merry dance she's led us!'

'You're welcome to her,' said Janssen. 'She's nothing to do with me.'

Mr Sharp stepped forward. 'Constable, I'm delighted to see you. I have here a writ from the magistrate which I am having some difficulty in executing. As you'll see, it expressly states that the person named below must present himself before the magistrate with one Pedro Hawkins – a boy who he has been holding against his will.'

Hawkins growled, 'It's none of his business. Let the man get on with his job.'

'As an officer in the employ of the said magistrate,' continued Sharp loudly, 'it is, of course, your duty to see that the writ is carried out to the letter.'

Constable Lennox read the writ through, a frown on his brow. 'And where do I find Mr Kingston Hawkins?'

'Fortunately, he is at hand, sir,' said Mr Sharp, gesturing to Pedro's old master. 'And I'm sure the magistrate will be most interested in the African boy's testimony for it will show that Mr Hawkins lied under oath when he said he had no knowledge of the child's whereabouts. That is perjury and punishable by a severe prison sentence, as I'm sure you know. Oh yes, and we will also be lodging a charge of attempted murder by Mr Hawkins when he attacked that girl there, an incident witnessed by all now present, including this lady, her grace, the Duchess of Avon.'

'You see, constable,' said the duchess in clarion tones, 'you thought you'd caught our little cat and you've come away with a tiger in the bargain.'

'This is preposterous!' spluttered Hawkins. 'I'm not going back with that clown!'

The Bow Street runner did not like the implication that he was in any way ridiculous. He puffed up his chest and faced Mr Hawkins, the highly polished brass buttons of his uniform glinting in the lantern light. 'Oh, but you are, sir. This writ is binding. I have no choice but to take you – by force if you will not come quietly. I take the girl too, of course,' Lennox added with evident satisfaction. Two arrests in one night would look good on his record sheet.

'Indeed, you must do your duty, constable,' said Mr Sharp. 'We will all come with you. But you may find on arrival at the court that Mr Hawkins will wish to drop his charge of assault against Miss Royal here when it is weighed against a counter-charge of attempted murder.'

Reluctantly, I left my friends and crossed the deck to surrender myself up to the runners. Two of them seized my arms tightly, determined not to let me give them the slip again. They chained my hands, Reader, but of course left that so-called *gentleman*, Hawkins, unfettered. He was escorted first to the boat. As I waited for my turn, Shepherd appeared at my side.

Frank and Charlie were with me in an instant.

'Pssst! Moggy,' hissed Billy. 'Tell your bulldogs to back off. I only want a quick word.'

He was hardly going to try anything surrounded by so many officers of the law. I gave
Frank and Charlie a nod.

'It's all right. I'd better hear what he has
to say.'

Reluctantly they moved off, remaining
within call.

'Looks like you'll be back 'ome soon, don't it?'
said Billy, leaning with his elbows on the rail,
gazing back at the lights of the city. 'I told
'Awkins I 'ad me money on you rather than 'im.'

'Thanks for your vote of confidence,' I
said sourly.

'That's all right, Moggy. You were just grand.
It was worth the trip out 'ere to see you shove
that mop in 'is face. Shame I won't be joining you
tonight in the lock-up: I do so enjoy our little
chats down there.' He jingled my chains. 'You
ain't forgotten, 'ave you?'

'Forgotten what?'

'Our bargain.'

Of course I hadn't. The thought filled me

with dread. My promise would still be hanging over me even if I did escape gaol. I was bound by my word, not only for my own honour, but also because I knew that, if I didn't keep it, Billy's game with me would be over and he'd most likely do away with me. I was stuck with the bargain I'd made. 'Billy, can't you just leave me alone? I promise I'll never come near you again.'

Giving me an enigmatic smile, he reached out and gave a tug on one of my curls. I flinched back and he took his hand away. 'I kept it,' he said and felt in his jacket pocket. I thought for a moment that he was going to pull a knife on me. 'Nah, Cat, it's not what you think. I kept this.' He held out a long lock of hair – my hair – the piece he'd shaved off almost a year ago.

'That's sick, Billy,' I said in disgust.

'When I want you to come, I'll send you this to let you know it's time. See you, Cat.'

And with that, he turned on his heel, climbed over the side to his boat and began to row for shore, humming to himself.

Miss Miller approached me. 'That young man is the devil incarnate, Sister Catherine. Thou must have nothing to do with him.'

'You're right – he's Satan himself,' I murmured. And, like the foolish Dr Faust, I appeared to have struck a dangerous bargain with him.

SCENE 3 – THE PRICE OF FREEDOM

By the time we arrived back ashore, we found the fish market had been transformed into a battleground. Groaning bodies and blood were strewn across the snow, splashes of scarlet on what had been glistening white. Milly and the younger Miss Millers were ministering to the injured, picking their way across smashed crates and crunching over oyster shells.

'What on earth's been happening here?' asked Mr Equiano.

'It was the mob from the Rookeries,' explained Milly, wiping her own cut lip with a lace handkerchief. Charlie hastened to her side but she waved him away. 'It's nothing – I just caught an elbow in the face. They were lying in wait for the Butcher's Boys – but we won.' She smiled, then winced as her lip began to bleed again.

I now noticed that among the fallen were several liveried footmen as well as Elias Jones. He had a nasty knife wound to his cheek.

'Is anyone seriously hurt?' asked Lizzie anxiously as the runners began to move among the injured, checking them over.

'Fortunately, no. It was mainly fists until an ugly thug arrived just before you landed. He had a knife. He slashed at anyone in reach, then whistled and the whole gang moved off, carrying their injured away.'

Constable Lennox gave a nod to two of his men. 'See if you can catch up with them and make sure you arrest that one with the knife.'

I knew it was too late. Shepherd would have disappeared back into the Rookeries. They had no more chance of catching him than trapping water in their hands. But Lennox had to look as if he were doing something before a duchess.

'How's Syd?' I asked, not seeing him among the boys on the ground.

My answer was a bone-crushing hug from behind. 'I'm all right, Cat,' he said. I wasn't so sure: his nose looked as though it was broken.

He had a puffy black eye and his clothes were in tatters. 'I'm just relieved to see you and Prince alive. I thought Shepherd 'ad trapped you both good and proper. I was near desperate to get out on the water but 'e 'ad all 'is boys waitin' for us.'

'You should have seen Mr Fletcher, Cat,' said Milly. 'He laid about him with his fists like a second Samson.'

'And you were pretty 'andy with that there umbrella of yours, if you don't mind me sayin', miss,' said Syd.

Milly blushed but looked very pleased at the compliment.

'But your nose, Syd?' I asked.

'Oh that? That's nothink. Got that earlier in the boxin' match. I'd just knocked 'im down when this lady strode into the ring, bold as brass, and told me what was up. You should've seen our faces. Never seen a lady at a fight before – except you, of course, Cat, but not a real, genuine top notch lady.'

'Thanks, Syd,' I muttered.

'You know what I mean, Cat. Anyways, I'll get me nose fixed when we get you 'ome.'

'I can't go home just yet. I'm under arrest.'

'Not again?' Syd groaned.

'But not for long, we hope,' added Pedro, coming forward to shake Syd's hand. 'So Shepherd didn't want you to come to my rescue. Then why tell Cat where I was?'

Syd shrugged. 'I guess 'e wanted to trap 'er too. What d'you think, Cat?'

I didn't want to let on to them about the deal I had struck with Shepherd. They wouldn't approve. 'I think it was his idea of fun,' I said lightly. 'He wanted to see if I could free you on my own.'

'He's evil,' commented Lizzie, shaking her head.

'Not all evil,' demurred Pedro quietly. 'He was the only one who was half-decent to me during my captivity. He brought Cat to see me, remember?'

'But he was the one keeping you locked up!' Lizzie protested.

'It wasn't personal,' Pedro said philosophically.

I agreed with Pedro: Billy was rotten but he had never had anything against my friend. Indeed, I had an inkling that Billy may have treated him well because he knew I cared for him. But that wasn't a pleasant thought. It reminded me too sharply of the complicated feelings Billy had for me, and standing here in the snow knowing that I had him to thank for saving Pedro, I knew that my attitude to him had become equally entangled. I hated him, of course, despised his way of life, naturally, but now there was a slight suggestion of gratitude, a glimmer of admiration for his diabolical cleverness in getting what he wanted from both Hawkins and me.

The runners commandeered hackney carriages to transport their two prisoners and the wounded back to Bow Street. Unfortunately, this meant I had to leave my friends to ride with the guards and Mr Hawkins. The slaver glared at me the whole way, no doubt wondering what revenge he could exact despite everything. I knew my weak spot even if he didn't: Pedro. Hawkins was still technically my friend's master. If Pedro stepped beyond the protection of his English allies, most courts around the world would hand him over to Hawkins without a second thought. Our victory in preventing Pedro's removal from England was only partial. He would still be living in fear of Hawkins for the rest of his life.

'Here we are, sir, miss,' said Constable Lennox, opening the door of the carriage.

We filed directly into the courtroom – no night in the holding cell for a gentleman of Mr Hawkins' standing. I was grateful for that. Sir John Solmes, the magistrate, had roused himself from his bed to meet us, wig askew, his eyes sleepy. I looked around in consternation: my friends had not yet arrived. I didn't want to face him on my own and I didn't like the feeling of being the only girl standing among all these great tall gentlemen. In my experience, there was some kind of secret understanding rich men shared.

I was not of their sex, nor even of their class: I was therefore beneath their notice.

'What's all this?' the magistrate barked at his constable. 'A Quaker maid in chains and a gentleman – why are they here at this time of night?'

'I brought the gentleman in compliance with this writ, sir,' said Lennox, handing over the *habeas corpus*. 'As for the girl – she's no Quaker. It's Cat Royal. You remember her, I think, sir.'

The magistrate rubbed his eyes and took a closer look at me. 'Oh yes, I remember her very well. Has a taste for disguise this one. What is the charge? Can I commit her straight to Newgate and be done with it?'

Newgate! I didn't fancy my chances of survival beyond a few weeks if I was pitched into that prison. It was an evil place by all accounts – a place of violence, squalor and misery.

'It was assault, sir, against the gentleman here,' said Lennox.

'Good, good,' said the magistrate, reaching for his gavel.

'Hold, man!' cried the duchess, flattening two runners behind the doors as she forced her way into the courtroom. Lizzie, Frank, Syd, Nick, Mr Equiano and Mr Sharp all followed. 'Tell your flunkies to admit us. This is supposed to be a public hearing.'

'Ah, your grace,' said the magistrate, looking at her with a fearful expression. I guessed he had already met her earlier that evening and had reason to tremble under the lash of her tongue. 'Of course you must come in. Do take a seat. We will not be long.' And he raised his gavel again.

'Wait!' said the duchess. 'You've not heard the counter-charge against this man on behalf of the girl.'

'Your grace, I am sorry to inform you that you must not speak out of turn. This is a court of law,' the magistrate said tentatively, the gavel drooping in his hand.

'Then when is it my turn? Surely not after you've dispatched the child to prison?'

'Er, of course not. She is entitled to representation in her defence.'

'Then *I* am her defence. Can I speak now?'

Frank and Lizzie grinned at me, for once completely unembarrassed by their mother's forthrightness. If I hadn't been so worried, I would have enjoyed it too.

The magistrate coughed awkwardly. 'It's most unorthodox,' (the duchess raised an eyebrow in warning), 'but, yes, your grace, you may speak.'

The duchess bustled to the front of the courtroom and laid her ermine muff on his desk. Her be-ringed fingers glittered dazzlingly in the candlelight. It struck me now that the opposite sex probably banded together in their gentlemen's clubs because they were plain scared of viragos like the duchess. She was like Athena, goddess of wisdom and warfare, come to shake the mere mortal men out of their complacency.

'I believe two charges are laid against Miss Royal – one for damages by the proprietor of Brooks, the other by this man who claims the accused bit him.'

Sir John nodded.

'The damages to the club will be paid by the Duke of Avon – double if need be. As for the alleged assault, I wish to say in her defence that the man in question was humiliating her and holding her against her will – shameful conduct for a gentleman whose duty it is to protect the weaker sex.'

Weaker sex? She must be joking. It was Sir John who was trembling before her.

'But that is all as nothing when set alongside the events of this evening when the same man, before many witnesses, including myself, tried to run her through with a sword.'

The magistrate let go of his gavel. 'Is this true?' he asked Hawkins.

The slave owner gave a shrug. 'She got in my way,' he said. 'Someone should've drowned the brat at birth – she's always in the way.'

Mr Sharp stepped forward. 'You may like to offer Mr Hawkins the chance to drop his charge against Miss Royal in return for Miss Royal dropping the charge of attempted murder. Not an entirely fair exchange, but one which should be to the advantage of both parties.'

The magistrate scratched his chin. 'What say you, Mr Hawkins?'

'I'll drop the charge,' Hawkins conceded in a resentful tone.

'Well, that seems to settle that then. Case dismiss–'

'No!' I interrupted. 'You haven't asked me yet. And I'm not dropping my charge against him.'

'Cat!' hissed Pedro. 'It's the only way!'

I steeled myself. 'No, it isn't. I accuse Mr Kingston Hawkins of attempted murder,' I repeated loudly.

My friends murmured among themselves, alarmed at my rashness. A sardonic smile curved

Hawkins' lips like the slash of a knife.

'The bantling wants to fight it out, does she?' he sneered.

'I do. What's the maximum penalty for a bite? Gaol with hard labour?' The magistrate nodded. Neither of us added that this was tantamount to a death sentence for puny mortals like me. I had to pretend I thought I'd survive for this to work. 'But for attempted murder – I'd say that's worth the gallows or transportation at the very least. No slaves to make your life comfortable in Botany Bay from what I hear. You'd be under a harsh master there yourself on the chain-gang. It'll do you good.'

Hawkins flicked his gaze from my face to the stern expression of the magistrate. The law officer said nothing to contradict my words.

'What do you want?' Hawkins snarled at me.

'Pedro's freedom – here and now, before all these witnesses.'

My friends gasped. Pedro stared at me in amazement.

'No!' Hawkins was white with fury. 'You're not getting that from me.'

'That's what I want. If you won't give it to me, I'll happily do my stint in gaol just to know you'll be out of Pedro's way for many long years and perhaps forever.'

There was silence as we all waited for Hawkins' decision. My heart was thumping. Pedro's knuckles were white on the bar beside me.

'All right!' Hawkins said at last. 'You can have his freedom. He's worthless to me now in any case.'

I felt a huge wave of relief. Pedro was free of him. I looked Hawkins in the eye and grinned. 'But not to me. To me, he's priceless. I drop my charge.'

The magistrate's gavel fell. 'Case dismissed.' Sir John leaned forward and surprised me by giving Pedro an avuncular smile. 'Oh, and if our Ariel so wishes, I would be honoured to stand godfather to his freedom. I have a nice big seal that no one will dispute.'

It was the last place I'd expected it, but clearly we had found another fan.

Cheers erupted from all quarters of the courtroom. Even Constable Lennox was seen to throw his hat in the air. Though disappointed in failing to nail me again, he still had the decency to enjoy the rescue of one of Covent Garden's favourite sons. Papers duly witnessed, Syd and Nick hoisted Pedro on their shoulders and led the procession back to Drury Lane. We had the good fortune to arrive just as the audience were leaving the performance. When the word spread as to what was afoot, scores joined the celebration, returning to the theatre for the impromptu party. Pedro was carried into the Pit, passed over the heads of the orchestra and placed centre stage next to Mr Kemble. The roof rang with whistles, cheers and applause. Pedro bowed and bowed – he'd never received such a standing ovation despite his previous triumphs. The crowd refused to give up.

Jostled aside by some eager spectators, I stood by one of the exits. Tears of joy streamed down my face as I saw Pedro had finally come home.

EPILOGUE

PIGEONS

Christmas Eve. Pedro and I were standing in the centre of Covent Garden, watching the snowflakes fall. The stalls were busy with shoppers buying their festive meal. Wreaths of holly and mistletoe decorated the doorways; candles brightened the windows. Across the square, the stained glass of St Paul's Church shone like jewels; the organist was playing out a jubilant carol.

'Cat, I want you to be the first to know,' Pedro announced.

'Know what?'

'My new name. You didn't expect me to stay Pedro Hawkins, did you?'

'I suppose not. So what have you chosen?'

Pedro hugged his arms to his side. 'It's better than that. I think I've rediscovered my true name.'

'How?'

'Mr Equiano. When I told him about my family – about my father being a king – he asked around among the African brothers and they came up with the answer. He thinks I'm probably an Amakye. I'm keeping Pedro – Mr Equiano told me it means "rock" and I was the rock that Mr Hawkins hit so that seems fitting. So Pedro Amakye it is.'

'Pedro Amakye. I like it.'

'So do I.'

Looking at my friend, free of the burden of slavery for the first time in his life, standing in the centre of London, his adopted home, I felt an exuberant joy bubble up inside me. We had to mark the moment. 'Well, we'll need to baptise you then,' I said pulling him towards the church.

Pedro frowned. 'I've been done once. I don't think they'll do it again.'

I began to laugh. 'Then it will have to be in snowflakes. See if you can catch one on your tongue.'

Pedro snuggled down inside his fur-lined cloak – his Christmas gift from Signor Angelini who understood what it was like to come from a warmer climate. 'That's a strange baptism. My tongue'll freeze.'

'Chicken!' I stuck my tongue out and caught a fat flake on its tip. 'Mmm, angel food!'

'Not very satisfying – I prefer hot meat and puddings,' he said, thinking of the feast that was being prepared for us in Grosvenor Square after his last performance as Ariel tonight.

'Try it!' I urged him. 'You might like it.'

'If *you* ask me, anything.' Pedro grinned and stuck out his tongue. 'De-licious!'

'What does it taste like?'

He linked arms with me. 'It tastes of . . . of friendship, of freedom – it's iced Bach, melting Mozart – and all things wonderful!' He began to whirl me round until it seemed that we were the only still things in the spinning world. 'It tastes of a new start, of dazzling success – it's Pedro Amakye.' He let go and I pirouetted on the ice before collapsing in a dizzy, laughing heap.

Giving me a tug to my feet, he began to run towards a flock of cold pigeons huddled together in the centre of the piazza. 'Come on, Cat! Now the baptism's over, let's see how far we can slide!'

With a shriek, we hurtled into the flock, arms flailing, shoes skidding. Startled, the pigeons flapped into the air and circled out to the boundless skies.

To the elements be free, and fare thou well.

Curtain falls.

CAT'S GLOSSARY

ARTICLES OF APPRENTICESHIP – agreement drawn up with a master to teach a boy a trade

BACK SLANG IT OUT OF SOMEWHERE – to make a rapid exit

BALDERDASH – a load of rubbish

BAMBOOZLE – to outfox, pull the wool over someone's eyes

BANTLING – a brat, an illegitimate child

BARNABY DANCE– an odd shuffle, like a couple of dancing jesters

BASKET OF CHIPS – a broad grin

BEAK – magistrate (to be avoided at all costs)

BILLINGSGATE – fishmarket on the north bank of the Thames

BLACK-BALLED – excluded, cut out – the members in gentlemen's clubs use a system where a white ball means you're voted in, black out. Dr Juniper is certainly a candidate for black.

BOW STREET RUNNERS – the magistrate's men who police the streets around Westminster (not my favourite people)

BREECHES ROLE – girls playing boys on stage

BROOK'S – an exclusive *gentlemen's* (though I have my doubts about some of its members) club known for its gambling

CANISTER – head (and some of us have a lot more in our canisters than others)

CANTING CREW – informal society of thieves with its own code of honour

CAPITAL TOPPER – top-rate drinker

CARD SHARP – someone who's handy with the pack, a professional trickster

CLAPHAM – village on outskirts of London, home to many abolitionists

CLOUGH'S – my boarding house at Westminster School

TO CUT A CAPER ON NOTHING – dance of death on the scaffold

TO DIE DAMNED HARD AND BOLD AS BRASS – praise often given to a condemned person's brazen attitude on the scaffold

FAG – a kind of schoolboy skivvy

FLASH – showy, rich

TO FLING ONE'S CAP AFTER – to make a hopeless appeal for something

GADSO – ah yes, oh dear, sorry about that . . . see within for Frank's explanation

GOOD PASTING – to be well and truly beaten (and don't I know how it feels!)

TO HOP THE TWIG – to get going

HOYDEN – boisterous girl (a term that's been applied to me – I can't think why . . .)

JARVEY – hackney cab driver

LIGHTER – flat-bottomed boat used to ferry cargo to and from ships

MIDDLE PASSAGE – second leg of three-part trading voyage that takes slaves from Africa to the West Indies

MONIKER – name, title

NAN BOY – a boy about whom you entertain doubts as to his manliness

NOUS – intelligence, knowledge

OTTLEY'S – a second-rate boarding house at Westminster School

PANTHEON – a ballroom, now on the slide (especially since Billy bought into it)

PISSPOT BULLY – small-scale, vulgar bully (an accurate description of Richmond, don't you think?)

THE PIT – lowest level in the theatre, frequented by gentlemen and those aspiring to be counted in that class

THE POOL – moorings in the Thames

POPPYCOCK – rubbish, nonsense

QUEER COVE – strange gent

RATS' CASTLE – decrepit building in middle of the Rookeries

ROOKERIES – also known as St Giles, a desperate and dangerous place

RUM 'UN – odd person

SHADOW – new boy looked after by a 'substance' or older boy at school

SKIVVY – me most of the time – downtrodden maid of all work

STOCK-IN-TRADE – what one does for a living

SUBSTANCE – older boy sponsor at school

THEATRE ROYAL, DRURY LANE – the best theatre in the world. And my home, just off Covent Garden

TENTER GROUND – place for stretching out cloth

TRAP – magistrate's man (NB also to be avoided)

VAPOURS – fainting fit, to be overcome, hysterical (NB only for rich girls)

WESTMINSTER SCHOOL – supposedly a place of learning for young gentlemen; in truth a den of floggers and bullies

WIPE – handkerchief

DEN OF THIEVES

THE THIRD VOLUME IN THIS CAPTIVATING SERIES IN WHICH Cat Royal JOURNEYS TO PARIS!

L'Opéra de Paris

*Will present today, Saturday 25 June 1791
the première of the ballet*

The Den of Thieves

PRINCIPAL DANCERS

MLLE. CAT ROYAL – English spy

'MILORD' FRANK AVON – Aristocrat on the run

M. JEAN-FRANCOIS THILAND – diminuitive king of the
Palais Royal Vagabonds

M. IBRAHIM – Bishop of the Notre-Dame Thieves

*In which the French Royal family flee as
Cat takes her first steps as a dancing spy.
She experiences the highs and lows of life in
revolutionary Paris and witnesses the
power of the people.*

VIVE LA REVOLUTION!